PIRATE: A WINGS OF DIABLO MC NOVEL- NEW ORLEANS CHAPTER

RAE B. LAKE

DISCLAIMER

This book includes several graphic traumatic events that may be troubling/triggering for some readers. Discretion is advised.

CHAPTER

1

Pirate

FIVE YEARS EARLIER

"Why are you acting like this, Delia? I thought you'd be happy to hear that they will let me prospect. Shit like this doesn't usually happen." I lean across the table and look at the rage growing on Delia's face.

"Happy!" Her voice takes on a feverish pitch.

It'll only be a few seconds before she loses her shit completely. I didn't think that she'd be upset.

I put my hand up for the server. If I know anything about my wife, it's that once she goes into one of her rages, there is no stopping her. Mario's is one of the nicest restaurants in the neighborhood. I'd hate to be banned from a place like this.

"How the hell could you ever think that I'd be happy about something like this? You just got out of the fucking military! Now you want me to be happy about the fact that you're going to join another band of brothers while I'm stuck on the fucking couch waiting for you to come home? Fuck you Jimmy! I don't have to deal with this shit!"

I bite my tongue and sit back in my chair as her voice escalates. If I try to calm her down, it'll only get worse. I look over to the waiter again who is standing on the other side of the room with the bill in his hand, staring at the drama unfolding at our table.

This was supposed to be a romantic night out, but just like always, any time Delia is unhappy the entire day turns to shit.

"What the fuck are you staring at! Bring me the damn bill!" I roar out and everyone jumps in surprise.

The waiter rushes over to me and hands me the bill. I take out a hundred and put it in the leather folder. We weren't even here long enough for our dinner to come. We've only had appetizers so far. Thank fuck for that, Lia ordered the steak. I don't want to know what the hell she'd do with a serrated knife.

I push away from the table and walk out, not really giving a fuck if she's behind me or not. We've only been married about two years and every time I think that we're getting to a better place, this shit happens again. It's like I'm dealing with a wild animal instead of a woman that's supposed to love me.

I step out onto the sidewalk and something hard hits me in the back before the sound of glass breaking filters through the air. I turn and duck just in time to see a wine glass being hurled at my head.

"You fucking pussy! I hate you! You never take care of me!" Delia screams at me as she picks up another glass, getting ready to throw this one at my head as well. I rush over to her and snatch it out of her hand before she has the chance to throw it.

If the cops are called, they'd haul her off to jail. I don't know how she hadn't been locked up yet in her life. Not with all the fucked up shit she does.

"Delia, what the fuck is your problem! All I do is fucking take care of you!" I grab hold of her hands and lock them down at her sides.

"How can you take care of me if you're never here? I'm always alone Jimmy."

I open my mouth to answer, but I can't tell her she's lying. I was in the army for twelve years, so I'm used to always being on the move. I had met Delia while I was on leave and even from the start, our relationship has been explosive. I've never been so addicted to a woman like I'm addicted to Lia. No one speaks to me like she does. No one touches me like she does, and honestly, no one fucks me like she does.

"Lia, I have to work. I want to be with you the same way you want me to be with you. But if I don't go out and make money, we don't fucking survive. We're not fucking rich." I let go of her hands and take a step back. There's a growing crowd around us. Spending a night in jail for domestic violence isn't something I look forward to.

"Money, money, money! That's all you fucking care about. You think I give a shit if we live in a studio apartment? Or if we have a new car. I don't fucking care about money Jimmy." She flips her hand in my face and scoffs, "I don't even know why the fuck I'm wasting my fucking time with you. You don't give a shit, anyway."

She storms away, and I take a few deep breaths before I follow. I know how this night ends, with one of us in tears.

DELIA SLAMS the door to our one-bedroom apartment. It's a third-floor walkup, but it's an acceptable distance from downtown. It's safer than anything else that we could find on my budget.

I put my forearm up so the door doesn't hit me in the face. I didn't bother to engage her outside when there was a chance that she would lash out at someone in her path just because they fucking looked at her wrong.

"Lia, can we just talk about this? I don't have the energy to fight with you tonight." I walk in and close the door behind me. "I didn't tell you about the club to piss you off. I told you, because I thought you'd understand—"

"Understand? No, I don't fucking understand how you can be okay with running behind a bunch of people you don't know just because you all served in the military. I don't understand how you would want to run around in an all boys club just because it's something to do. You're a fucking piece of shit Jimmy and I don't want anything to do with whatever the fuck you have going on."

"I'm a piece of shit? I know them. I served with Jameson. If he says these guys are on the up and up, why would I not want to be with them? Or do you want me at a regular nine to five? You'd rather we scrape by and still never see each other. At least with the club you have someplace to be safe. You can be with me there. It's not like me being deployed." I try to explain, but she's already staring off into space. Nothing is sinking in and my chest clenches with frustration.

"If they call while you're with me, do you stay or do you go?" She asks suddenly.

"I'd go, the same way a police officer or a firefighter would," I say instantly.

"Then that is where we have our problem. Don't you think, I want to be first in all fucking things?"

"You are fucking first, Delia! How can you not see that? This is my chance to make sure you have everything you need. It's my chance to be a part of something I know I'm good at and still have you there with me. God damn it, why does everything have to be so fucking hard with you. All the time. Just for once I'd like to come to you with something and you not act like a fucking crazy bitch about it." I'm tired of her selfishness, of having to explain in the most sugar-coated detail why I'm doing things that would better our life.

"You want to see a crazy bitch! I'll show you crazy!" She screeches and like a fucking angry wild animal, she comes barreling towards me.

I put my hands up to block her blows, but for someone so small, the girl packs a punch. She pops me twice in the face and stars erupt behind my eyelids. I try to grab her hands, but she bites my forearm hard enough for me to scream out in pain.

"Fuck! Stop! What the fuck are you doing?" I push her back, and she stumbles down to her ass. "Delia! Fucking stop this shit. I don't want to hurt you!" I warn her. I'd leave before I strike her, but I know I can't walk out on her in this state.

She stands back up and saunters over to me. She's out of breath. Her honey-blonde hair is plastered to the side of her face and the back of her neck—she's sweating so much. Delia is a solid five-six, but she's still much shorter than my six-one height, so she cranes her neck back and stares directly into my eyes, daring me to react. "Hurt me then Jimmy. I don't think you have the fucking balls to do shit to me. You're just going to run away like you always fucking do. Pussy!" She's in my face, but at least she's not swinging at me anymore.

"Watch your fucking mouth, Delia. I'm not a fucking pussy. This shit gets us nowhere and you know it." I can feel the tension crackling around us. The flames raging out of control in both of us—lust, need, anger.

She pushes me against the wall hard enough for the picture to rattle, "It gets your cock in me."

My eyes hone in on her mouth and the second she mouths the words 'fuck me,' any type of willpower I thought I might have had is gone. My hands fly to her neck and I push her back to the other wall where I slam my mouth against hers. My tongue fighting its way into her mouth. She captures my bottom lip between her teeth and bites down hard.

"Fuck!" I roar out and rip my mouth away from her. Blood trickles down my chin. I grab hold of her hair and turn her away from me. I push her hard against the wall and tear the thin shirt she is wearing away from her body. She gasps and pushes with her knee against the wall so we go flying back.

I hold on to her with one arm to make sure she doesn't hurt herself and use the other hand to brace our fall. My back collides with the ground and it forces the air out of my lungs. It's like a twelve-round fight with this woman when we fuck. All I know is by the time it's over I may look like I went the distance with the champ, but I always come out a winner.

She turns over and claws at my button-down shirt. I had tried to dress a little fancy tonight since we were going out to celebrate. I should have stuck with my typical black t-shirt. Buttons go flying everywhere as she rips the shirt open. Her nails catch against my skin and leave a trail of welts in her wake. She rocks her core against my still-clothed dick and I stretch my head back, reveling in the feeling.

Delia suddenly stops moving and grabs hold of my face, digging her nails slightly into my chin. "This is what you're missing out on every time you fucking leave me. Since you want to go so bad, maybe you should start missing me now." She lifts herself off me and starts walking away. In the process, she pulls down the zipper on the side of her skirt and lets the fabric fall down her legs before she steps out of it and continues walking toward the bedroom.

"It may be a good thing you need to run off with your all-boys club. Maybe it's time I find someone to take care of me properly." She turns her head, so I can see her profile, but she keeps her eyes focused down. "Someone to take care of all of me." She shrugs and continues to walk.

I catapult myself off the floor and rush her. She turns just in time to see me barreling toward her. "You fucking bitch! Why you always doing this shit to me! This what you want! Huh? You want me going out of my fucking mind?" I pick her up and slam her against the wall right by our bedroom.

We have a small shelf near the bathroom with all Delia's girly shit since there's not much space in there. I slam her so hard against the wall the entire unit falls over, creating a slippery mess of body gel and lotion on the floor under us. It doesn't matter to me. Nothing besides the savior himself is going to stop me from showing my woman that there is no one else that is going to take better care of her than I will.

I shove my pants down barely enough to get my dick out and pull her panties to the side. There is no checking to see if she's ready, no soft kisses or sweet caresses. She screams out as I enter her, but I don't know if it's in pain or pleasure. I like to think I'd be able to stop if she told me to right now, but she's never told me to stop no matter how rough we get with one another.

I ram into her hard, and she moans loud, digging her nails into my shoulders and cursing my name every few thrusts until she comes gloriously on my dick. I'm not finished with her, though. She may have gotten her release, but I'm still as wound up as I was when we'd walked through the door. I rush her to the bedroom and drop her on the bed while I push the rest of my clothing off.

Out of breath and still coming down from her orgasm, Delia still tries to dig into me. "You ready to give this up, Jimmy? You can't keep up anymore, can you?"

"Shut up! Shut the fuck up. I don't want to hear that bullshit." My voice is rough and booming. I'm a large man and would intimidate most people, but instead of Delia flinching she laughs at me.

"Of course you don't want to hear the truth!" She kicks out her foot and I have to bend away, or she'd connect her heel with my balls. I grab her ankle and use all the strength I have to turn her so she's face down in the bed. I bend her arms allowing me to secure her hands against her back and I use my knees to spread her legs open. Again, I push my way inside and her body accepts me. Her pussy's wet enough I can see her arousal glistening down her thighs.

I buck into her hard and fast, growling and grunting like an animal racing towards my release. I pound into her until the sweet agony of my climax erases every thought from my mind. My toes curl and my muscles bunch up as my balls squeeze up tight and I explode deep inside of her.

I pull out of her, not giving a fuck that a small stream of my cum drips out of her cunt and onto the sheets as I do. I lay on my back and stare up at the white popcorn ceiling. The apartment has some water damage and there are a few cracks that need to be taken care of. I've seen these same cracks for months. Usually after the same series of events. Lia gets mad about something, we argue, she fights me, and I fuck her. Then we lay here in peace for a few hours. Then the next day or the next week, it all happens again.

We might have met when I was still enlisted, but I've fought more wars with Delia in the year and a half that I've been with her. I thought once I got home things would be different. It just seems like things are getting worse.

I've tried to get her to go to a therapist to work out some of her anger, but that just escalates into a fight. I don't know what to do, but I know I can't keep up with all this turmoil.

"Lia, this has to stop." I say, my voice thick with shame and emotion.

"I love you, Jimmy." She whispers, turning her head to look at me.

I turn to make eye contact with her, "We don't love the same."

"Does that make it wrong?" She asks, and I don't have an answer for her.

Our passion for each other is scorching hot and destructive. How can something that hurts as deeply as this be right? I can't see myself without her, but I don't see how either of us survive together.

CHAPTER

2

Pirate

PRESENT

"Gator, we need to figure out what we are going to put in now that the craps table is moving. It's just an open space now where we could make money." I walk through the north side of the casino that we are working on expanding. I had wanted them to put in a new floor, but with the sponsor program going on upstairs most nights, it just wasn't in the plans. The last thing we need is our elite clientele having to walk through another level of players in order to get to the bidding rooms. That wouldn't work out for anyone.

"We don't have enough dealers for more blackjack or poker. We could put in more slots, but it may throw off the flow." Gator sips on his drink while he talks to me, but he's not really paying attention to me.

Gator's usually as focused as I am when it comes to the casino, especially now that we are finally getting it back on its feet. The casino had been closed for a little while. The public thought it was closed for renovations. Except in reality the casino was closed since we were in a bloody war with not only the fucking Drift Demons, but also Rooster, René, and the Purged.

Now that the Purged and Rooster were taken care of, all we are on the lookout for is René and the Drift Demons. The threat is still great, but it's not enough that we have to keep everything shut down. It's time that we live our lives again.

As the treasurer for the club when the casino had to be closed down, I know how much money we were actually losing. It hurts just to complete the ledgers every week. Most times when people see a bunch of grizzly men on bikes, they think that's all that comes along with being in a MC, but that's far from the truth. We need money to live, money to make sure our members and their families are happy. Fuck we need money to make sure we stay safe. I'm ecstatic to have the doors to the casino open again.

Gator and Yang have been running around with me, trying to make more room to get unique attractions in here. Yang is on a run with Clay, so it's just Gator and I at the casino today. I had figured that we'd be out of here by now, but Gator can't seem to stay on task.

"What the fuck are you looking at?" I ask, finally fed up enough that I have to keep pulling his attention back to what we're doing.

"I'm looking at the two women that have been eye fucking us since we stepped on the floor. Instead of staring down at that pad of yours, maybe you should stop and smell the flowers every once in a while."

I look over his shoulder and see two women who sure enough, are giggling and staring at us. Both of them are sexy as fuck. I immediately find myself drawn to the woman with dark hair. She has it in a high pony-tail and my first thought is how many times could I get her hair wrapped around my fist.

She spies me watching her and crooks a finger at me, inviting me over. I really should finish the walk-through, but Gator is right. Sometimes it's nice to just stand back and enjoy the fruits of our labor. The women are never in short supply and once they find out that I'm a member of a MC, the panties usually come off even quicker. All the good girls want a quick fuck with a bad boy.

"Fuck it." I roll the papers I'm working on up and stuff them in my back pocket. I could do this shit when I get back to the clubhouse.

"You two having a good time?" Gator asks as we walk up to the two women.

"Absolutely, it's so awesome this place opened back up. It's my birthday, and I knew I had to come cele-brate it here." The one with the light hair says.

"Happy birthday!" I grumble out.

"Yeah, it's my twenty-first." The one staring at Gator replies.

"Twenty-one? That's a wonderful age." Gator drapes his arm around the giggling woman and starts laying the game on thick. I almost want to laugh. Twenty-one.

"So what do you boys do here?" The woman with the dark hair asks.

"Look sweetheart, I know you and your girlfriend are out to have a good time tonight. But I don't think I'm the right one to show it to you." I cross my arms over my chest and stare down at her as her smile turns into a cute pout. A cute, young-as-fuck pout.

"Why not? Did you want my friend or something?"

"No, it's nothing like that, but I'm not in your age range. You're a little young for me." I'm honest. At thirty-six, there is very little a twenty-one year old could do for me. Hell, if I'm honest, after being married to Delia, there isn't much anyone could do for me.

"I'm not young. I'm a big girl, and I like my men older. The more experience the better." She takes a step closer to me and pushes her shoulders back to show me the curve of her breasts.

She's trying way too hard.

"I'm not looking for a sugar baby or a girlfriend." I say keeping my face straight. It's been a while since I've had this type of release, so I'm fine with playing with her as long as she knows what she's getting herself into.

"I'm not looking for any of that either." She whispers.

"What do you want?"

She looks over her shoulder to see the people walking around behind her. She's embarrassed.

"I don't have time for shyness, either you know what you want or you don't." Being an asshole isn't required, but I will not sugarcoat this.

"I want you to take me some place private." She hisses up at me.

My eyes scan the crowd and I see Gator walking with the blonde towards the moon quarters. In that part of the compound, it's mostly self-care amenities. Spas and nail salons, things we know people are going to use after losing a bunch of money. Gator knows there are private rooms we can use in that area.

I guess he has the same idea I do. "Fine, after you." I put my hand out, gesturing in the direction that I want her to walk. She keeps her thumbs hooked into the belt loops of her jeans as we follow Gator and her friend.

"You don't do this type of thing often, do you?" I ask her when I see her searching the area.

"No. I'm not a virgin or anything like that if that's what you're worried about." She snaps at me as if what I'm saying is an insult.

"The only thing I'm worried about is you doing what you want to do. You don't have to do something just because your friend is doing it."

She huffs out a single note laugh, "Are you my father now?"

"Fuck no I'm not." I follow Gator and her friend into the room. He already has her pressed against the far wall, pawing at her breasts and kissing on her neck. It's very dim in the room, but I can make out what's going on. It's nothing new to me. I've seen pretty much all of my brothers fuck at some point until they find their ol' lady. The only one I haven't seen is Archer, because he had started this chapter with Daria.

The dark haired girl seems shocked that her friend is about to get railed right here in front of her. "You can leave anytime you want." I say as I sit on the couch, staring up at her.

The sound of bodies slamming into the wall lets me know Gator is already having a grand old time. Good for him.

"I don't want to leave." the girl says.

"But?" I say. My gut tells me she wants to have fun, but I'm not going to force myself on anyone. No one is worth that hassle.

"I don't want to fuck, I want to …" Her words trail off, but I see her lick her lips and stare down at my dick.

My eyebrow arches up, and I spread my legs, inviting her to do what she wants. "I'm not stopping you, beautiful."

She smiles at me genuinely for the first time since we had started walking together and kneels between my legs. She unbuckles my pants and I help her pull them down over my hips. My cock is only semi-hard, but even at half mast my size is nothing to sneeze at.

She jerks me softly a few times, "I'm not going to break." I tell her and she takes that as her cue to have fun. She leans over and sucks hard on the crown of my cock, causing me to buck up into her mouth.

"Mmm," I groan and my hand instinctively grabs hold of her ponytail. "Fuck, I like that shit."

She's sloppy, but enthusiastic. It's more than I was expecting from a shy girl who couldn't even voice that she wanted my cock down her throat.

It's not long before she tries to deep throat me and ends up gagging. That just causes me to surge forward. She pulls away and breathes deeply before dropping her head back into my lap and continuing. My head falls against the back of the couch as my body gears up to come.

Sparks shoot through my body and I know that any second a warm load is going to slide down this woman's throat. I give her the universal shoulder tap. "If you don't want me coating your stomach, fucking stop." I growl out, but she only doubles her efforts.

That's a good enough response for me.

I grip her head hard and proceed to fuck her face as deep as I want until a small rush of satisfaction comes over me. I come in three quick bursts, spilling my seed into her mouth and down her throat.

She swallows it all and uses her thumb to wipe the corners of her mouth. She stands and fixes her clothes, but doesn't say another word to me.

When I look around, I don't see Gator or the friend anymore. The two of them must already be finished. "You want to go catch up with your girlfriend?" I ask, stuffing my dick back into my pants.

"Yeah, I don't want to leave her alone." She replies and smiles softly.

"All right. Let's go then."

We leave the small dark room to see Gator texting on his phone. "Ah, you two finished?" When I nod he continues, "Your friend is in the bathroom over there."

"Great, thanks." She looks up at me and swipes her finger over her bottom lip. "For everything."

"My pleasure." I reply as she walks away.

I stretch my neck from side to side before I pull out the plans I have rolled up in my back pocket.

"Jeez, man, right back to work?" Gator shakes his head at me.

"What? Did you think I was going to be swooning over getting my dick sucked? Please." I scoff and continue looking over the sheets of paper in my hand.

"No, but fuck, could you at least look like you had some fun? Fuck, what does a girl have to do to impress you?" He asks and even though I don't answer him, I'm screaming a response in my head.

Lia is the only one that will ever impress me.

The woman ruined me for anyone else. The level of heat that we had for each other desensitized me to everyone else. Since her there's never been another and no matter how many club bunnies, good girls, and wifey material women my brothers throw at me, no one would ever compare.

All of them are good for a quick fuck or two, but none of them would ever be my Delia.

CHAPTER

Delia

"This is bullshit. If I wanted to take fucking drugs, I'd hit up the man on the corner. Who the fuck does she think she is!"

"Well, for starters, she's a doctor that has way more time studying the way the mind works than you, Lia. Maybe you need to listen to her or not. It's your life." Noah shrugs his shoulder and stops to look at himself in the glass storefront. The man is as metrosexual as I've ever seen. He spends more time in the bathroom getting ready than I do.

"The doctor at the ER said I didn't need to take any medication." I grumble out.

"Mhmm." Noah replies, but doesn't look at me.

"I'm sorry. Let me know when you're finished with your grooming session so we can address my life crisis," I snap at him and cross my arms over my chest. "For fuck's sake, you'd think you were waiting for a slut to hop out of the store display as hard as you're fucking looking at yourself."

He turns around and stares down at me. "Delia, you and I both know that there's nothing I can say that's going to change your mind about what you're going to do. You went into that therapy session knowing that you didn't want to take medication. Are you going to take it?" Noah asks, cutting straight through the bullshit.

"No." I answer immediately.

"Then what the fuck are we talking about it for?"

"Fuck you! You uptight, conceited bastard, God forbid, I take five seconds out of your fucking day to talk through my shit. Forget this and forget you!" I shove my finger against his forehead and push him back.

Noah doesn't race to follow me, he doesn't fight me back, he just lets me walk off. We've been through this long enough for both of us to know that my brain doesn't process anger like a normal person. I start at one and before I can hear what the other person tells me, I'm already at a thousand.

It's taken a few years of therapy for me to realize that most of the time the situation doesn't call for my level of anger. Right now is one of those times. I stop walking and turn around to see Noah still at the storefront, fixing his hair. He has a cowlick today that he can't quite get to go in the direction he wants it to go. If he weren't so particular about his hair, I'm sure he would have shaved his head already.

I walk back over to him and stand there, looking at his reflection and how jacked up my own is. "If you just went with it, you could look mussed up. Ladies like seeing a man that's just been fucked."

"Good fucking idea. Come on, pull on my hair."

"What?" I laugh, "No."

"Why not? You know you want to. Besides, you're the only one I trust with their fingers in my hair besides my hair dresser that is. Get those fingers in there and mess me up. Nicely though, if you please." He winks at me and leans down so his head is within reach.

"Ugh. You're ridiculous, you know that?"

"Nah, I'm just a sexy motherfucker."

"So fucking conceited." I slip my fingers into his hair and start tugging like I would if I were fucking him.

"Oh yeah, that's it, baby. Hurt me!" He moans loudly. A couple walking by stares at us and I burst out laughing. Noah is good for that. No matter what is going on by the end he has a smile on my face.

"Shut up!" I push him away once I'm finished, and he turns back again to the window.

"Yeah, much better." He combs the sides of his hair flat against his head, but leaves the top part of his hair a mess. Now instead of looking polished and put together, he looks like a rockstar who doesn't give a damn about his hair. It's bad on purpose. "Let's get out of here."

He drapes an arm over my shoulder and we continue down the block in the apartment's direction. Another reason Noah and I get along so well is because he doesn't dwell on my blow ups. I could have cursed him out to kingdom come and he just lets it roll off his back like I hit him with a fucking feather.

"I don't want to depend on anything. Ever." I admit to him. That's my base fear. It took me a long time to get clean.

"Lia, I understand. If anyone does, I do. If it were something recreational, I would tell you to not even think about it. But baby cakes, you've been awake for almost two weeks. An hour of sleep here and there isn't doing it. You're about to be dead on your feet. You need to at least restart your system." He says, finally looking at me.

"They're addictive, though. I mean my body will eventually force me to sleep right? I don't know if I can chance it." I chew on my bottom lip, thinking about my options.

After Jimmy and I got a divorce, my life literally went to shit. I ended up turning to drugs to take the edge off my anger, but all that did was make me angrier. I fought anyone without a care in the world until one of my fights put a woman in the hospital and the cops threw me in a jail cell.

I didn't even let them call Jimmy, I just laid there wishing to fucking die.

The judge gave me a slap on the wrist. He let me go as long as I agreed to detox and anger management. Forcing me to talk to someone about why I am so angry all the time was the best thing he could do for me.

Once I finished the court mandated therapy, I found more for myself and even joined some of the group therapy sessions. That's where I met Noah. It was like we were two kindred spirits right from the beginning. The shit I rolled my eyes at, he did as well. I knew from right then we were going to be inseparable. I was right, we've been around each other since that day.

I was living on my own until about two weeks ago when I found myself pinned under a man who didn't understand what get the fuck off me meant. Now every time I close my eyes, all I see is that bastard's face and I wake up screaming for help. My entire childhood was one traumatic episode after another, but this one I can't shake. Noah offered to let me stay with him until I felt safe or forever, his words not mine.

"How about you take like three days' worth so you get into some sort of pattern, then switch to the over-the-counter stuff? I just want you to take care of yourself, Delia. You're going to need medicine at some point in your life, you just have to have faith that you're not going to spiral back down into the hard shit. I'm going to be with you every step of the way." He kisses the side of my head and I lean into his embrace.

I believe him.

"Yeah, okay. I'll take like half to see if it even works. I just want to get some sleep that's not interrupted."

"I want that too. I mean, usually when a woman is screaming in my house it's because I'm fucking her brains out, not because of night terrors." Noah jokes and I elbow him in the gut.

Loud honking horns sound behind me, and my entire body freezes. I hear someone speeding up in our direction and the first thing I can think of is the man that raped me had come back to finish the job. In that split second, I feel fear all over again. Usually, I'm ready to fight anyone who dares mess with me, but I can't break out of the paralyzing anxiety that someone is going to hurt me again.

Noah quickly shoves me behind him, and for the briefest second all sounds stop except for one voice.

Jimmy.

CHAPTER

Pirate

I WILL ADMIT THAT I'M IN A BETTER MOOD SINCE I WAS able to blow my load down the dark-haired girl's throat. Only it didn't stop me from making sure all the plans were complete for what the club wants to do regarding the new games.

Gator had got the birthday girl's phone number. He's been texting her back and forth since the two of them left us and went about their day. We were literally just a way for them to have a good time. I don't mind being used for a woman's enjoyment, but I know when to cut shit off. Gator, on the other hand, does not. He's still pursuing the young woman like he's going to take her out on dates and shit like that.

"Can we get the fuck back home before you start having phone sex with her? I don't need to hear that shit." I grunt out.

"Oh, you're such a damn hater. You could have your-self a sweet little plaything if you ever fucked any of these girls more than once." Gator replies as he puts his helmet on and starts up his bike.

"Once is enough." I reply before I do the same.

The ride back to the clubhouse would take us only a few minutes. Besides, I'm eager to get back to Archer and the rest of the boys to let them know how many more tables we could fit in the main area if we consolidate the progressive slots.

Also, if we put in a sports betting area, we could really pull in a lot of bank. As far as I can tell, there are only a few places that offer it in the state and none of them are close to where we are located. I can't believe we didn't think of this before.

"Hey, sexy." I hear Gator's deep voice come through the in-helmet receiver.

"What the fuck?" I complain and quickly flick the switch so I don't have to hear him any longer. He's on the phone with that girl. Fucking ridiculous. I don't want to hear that shit.

I stay beside him, but I don't turn my headset back on. Riding in silence never bothered me before. The main road through town is pretty empty, so I'm not really worried about the Drift Demons rolling up on us. Since we took down Rooster, they have kept to themselves. I don't know where René is, but without Rooster, he seems to have lost all of his bravado.

I scan the area and see people walking around, just enjoying their day. A woman and her two kids stop at the crosswalk and wait for it to turn red again. A man's screaming into his phone, probably some deal at work gone bad. A couple walks down the block in a loving embrace and I watch him kiss his woman on her forehead.

My blood freezes in my veins as I squint and pay closer attention to the two of them. The woman has light blue hair and she's about five foot six. The swish of her hips seems familiar, too fucking familiar. That's my fucking woman.

I don't think before taking a U-turn into oncoming traffic. I hear Gator scream at me, but I don't care to wait for him. That woman is Delia and that bastard motherfucker is kissing up on her in public—in my goddamn face.

Cars blow their horns and a few have to skid to a stop so they don't collide with me. I jump the curb before I engage the kickstand and get off my bike.

The man pushes Delia behind him and stands tall like he's going to stop me from getting to her. He's tall, but he's thin like he's never seen a fucking dumbbell he liked in his life. His hair is fucked up and blond. He has on those thick, black, geek hipster glasses, and I think the bastard has on fucking suspenders. This man is definitely not my Lia's style.

"Who the fuck are you?" I growl out.

"Who the fuck are you, riding up on the damn sidewalk like a fucking madman?" Suspenders takes another step into my face.

I raise my eyebrow. Maybe he's not what he seems. Either way, I'm going to knock him the fuck out just for even breathing the same air as Delia.

"Motherfucker, I will not ask you again. Who the fuck are …" I glimpse over the skinny man's shoulder and see Delia standing there with her eyes squeezed shut like she is trying to get her breathing under control. I've never seen her like that, but what I'm more concerned about is the fucking shiner she's got under her eye. Did this asshole punch her in the face like that?

"You don't have anything to say now?" The man in front of me is still talking shit, but I've already seen all I need to know.

I pull my fist back and plow it right into the man's face. I try to break every bone in that pretty boy smirk of his. He takes the first blow and when I come back with another swing, he quickly ducks it and throws his own haymaker at my face. For a thin man there is power behind his punch, but I've been in way too many fights and I'm too pissed for anything he does to faze me.

Gator runs up behind me and pulls me off the thin man before I fucking kill him.

"Brother, what the fuck are you doing? It's broad daylight, and you got your fucking kutte on!" He whispers harshly in my ear.

He's right. If shit goes bad with this guy and I actually killed him, it'd blow back on the club and my family.

"Stop! Noah stop." Delia finally moves from where she is and pulls the man back as he tries to come at me again. "I'll handle this asshole. You go on home."

"Fuck that. The motherfucker put his mitts on me. I think I might want to break them the fuck off." The thin man threatens me, and I nearly lose my shit once again.

"I'd like to see you fucking try. Come a little closer so I can break that scrawny neck of yours." I yell back at him and Gator pulls me further away.

"Brother, you gotta cool out. You're causing a fucking scene."

When I look around again, we have an audience of pedestrians. I shake him off and turn back to see Delia telling whoever the fuck that man is that she is going to handle me.

"I'll be at the end of the block when you're done. If he steps out of line even a little, wave me over and I'll finish the fucking conversation for you." The man puts his hand on the back of her neck rubbing the skin there. Lia nods like she believes he might.

"You don't have to fucking wait for her signal, bitch. I'm right fucking here!" I pull out of Gator's grip, but Delia steps in front of me.

"And I'm right here! Who in the fuck do you think you are, Jimmy?" Delia screams in my face.

"Back up off me, woman." I take a step away.

"We don't need to be doing this shit here." Gator tries to pull me away again.

"I fucking got it! I'm good!" I yell at him and throw my hands up before I take a breath to calm down. "I'm good, Gator."

He backs away, but there is still a large group of people looking at us. My eyes scan the crowd. "Move the fuck on. The show is over." I snap at them and they all start moving.

"I don't know what the fuck you think you're trying to pull, but I don't have the time or the fucking strength for it." Delia hisses at me.

"Who did that to your fucking face?" I keep my voice low.

"This?" She points up to the black eye that I'm obviously talking about. "Now you give a fuck? I don't need you to stick your fucking nose in my business now, Jimmy. We're through, remember?" She smirks at me.

"I don't give a fuck if we're not married anymore Delia, I'm still going to take care of you."

"You're shit at your job Jimmy."

"Tell me who the fuck did it!" I yell.

"You don't need to worry about it. I don't need shit from you! I don't want nothing from you. Get away from me!" She puts her hands on my chest and shoves me.

"Lia, just fucking talk to me. I'm trying to help you." I grab hold of her shoulders, but she shakes me off and slaps me hard across the face.

"I don't want your help, Jimmy. Go back to your club and find out how you can be useful to them. Go be Pirate. Noah's got this." She squints at me, giving me a little smirk.

Jealousy and rage surges through me. Delia knows this. She's pushing my buttons. "Noah don't got shit!" I get closer to her.

I swear I hear the air sizzling around us. It's always like this.

Just as I'm about to say something else, my phone goes off. Delia scoffs and turns away, "Lia, wait!"

She walks backwards for a second, "Nah I'd rather not, besides mother is calling."

My phone goes off again and when I pull it out of my pocket, she's right. Archer is calling me.

I answer, "Yeah?"

"What the fuck am I doing watching you on a goddamn Facebook live post?" He barks into my ear.

Shit!

I turn in a circle and even though everyone around me has gone, there are still a few stragglers standing on the other side of the street. One of them must be recording me.

"My bad, prez. I saw— "

"I know who the fuck you saw, Pirate. Like I said, you're streaming live for the fucking world to see. All we need right now is another fucking target on our backs. Get your shit together, grab Gator and get the hell back to the damn clubhouse." He hangs up the phone before I get to say another word.

My eyes look down the block to see Delia under the arm of that skinny bastard yet again. I don't know who the hell did that shit to her face, but I know whoever did it would pay.

CHAPTER 5

Pirate

I RACE TO THE CLUBHOUSE NOT BECAUSE I'M IN TROUBLE. No, because I feel like following that piece of shit and putting a fucking bullet in his head.

I park my bike in my spot and walk into the clubhouse.

"Pirate, bring your fucking ass over here." Archer commands me as I take one foot over the threshold.

I walk over to where he is and though I know, physically, the man is smaller than me out of everyone in the clubhouse. He is the one I would say I fear the most. Not only since he's my president and on his word every one of my brother's would shoot me in the face, but he has a dominance about him I've never seen crack.

"Yeah, Prez?" I do my best to keep my tone respectful.

"Maybe I'm losing my damn mind, so I'll have you remind me. What did we all agree would be the best thing to do until we are totally clear of Bull and his asshole crew?" Archer stands in front of me and stares daggers straight through me.

"Keep a low profile."

"Right, that's what I thought we all agreed on. So is this shit keeping a low profile?" He lifts his phone to press play on the now old video of me and that Noah motherfucker fighting on the sidewalk. My Wings of Diablo kutte is clearly visible for all the world to see. I had made a fucking embarrassment out of myself.

"It's not. I fucked up. I'm sorry. I lost my head." I don't have any other excuse besides that.

"For fucking what, though? Because Delia was walking with another man? Brother, I understand you and her were married, but the both of you have moved on with your life. Did you think she'd never find another boyfriend?" Archer asks. Usually I'd tell anyone what goes on between Lia and me is none of their business, but Archer can make it his business.

"No, I mean yeah, I knew she'd get another man. She's beautiful, but I'm not going to stop making sure she's okay. I just can't fucking do it." I shrug and look down. The feeling of weakness floods through me. It's not every day I admit that I'm not fully over my ex.

"Is she okay?"

My eyes pop back up to my president, who is no longer looking at me like he's pissed. He has his own woman and though I know for sure that Daria would never leave him. Though if that were to ever happen, I don't think he'd ever let anything happen to her, either. "I don't know. I flipped out on the dude she was with, because she had a huge black eye."

"Bro, you know how she likes to fight. She could've gotten that shit anywhere." Jameson is the one to speak up.

"I know it, but I asked her. She would have told me she got it beating some bitch's ass, but she didn't and when I pulled up, she didn't jump straight into fight mode. It was like she was trying to stop herself from panicking. Lia doesn't fucking panic when shit gets crazy. She's like Harley Quinn. She laughs and runs headfirst into the fucking flames. I don't know if the skinny bastard hit her, but if he did I have to break his face."

"I hear you and if you think he's a danger to her, we'll get it worked out." Archer claps a hand on my shoulder to let me know that he still has my back.

"You want me to go pay him a visit? I'm sure I can get the right answers out of him." Bones offers up, but I shake my head no.

If anyone is going to beat Noah down for putting his hands on my Lia, it'd be me.

"No, if it needs to be done, I want to be the one to do it. Yang, could you do me a solid?" I call over to my brother, who is sitting with his woman in his lap.

"Name it."

"You're better at this social media stuff than I am. I saw a bunch of tags on the post, but my mind isn't in the right place to sort through it all. See if you can find a profile or any information on him. His name is Noah, I just want to see what he's about."

Yang nods his head and pulls out his phone, already on task.

I stand there in the middle of the floor while the rest of my brothers walk off going about their business. Everything is fine now, but instead of me coming down from this rage fueled high, I feel like my body is stuck in fight mode.

I need to get rid of this extra energy. I find myself walking towards the back rooms in the clubhouse hoping Lex is up for a few rounds. I knock a few times and he opens the door quickly, a book in his hand and his reading glasses on his face. He's the only one in the clubhouse that is older than me, but in hand to hand combat he is the most lethal.

Lex was a legit contender until he'd figured out that he needed to find a way to take care of his little girl, then he went into the underground circuit where he was the champ for years. A bad run in with René and he wound up here with us after his daughter and my VP became a pair. He may not fight professionally any more, but the man throws sledgehammers for fists. He's a great sparring partner.

"You good Pirate?"

"Not really. You think you could spar with me for a little bit. I need to beat on something." I admit to him, and he smirks at me.

"You mean you need to swing at air while I knock you on your ass? Sure. Give me a minute to get my gear, I'll meet you out there." He takes his glasses off and puts his book down before he turns to get his stuff. I go up to my room to get my own and pray that this little boxing session would be enough to calm myself down.

AN HOUR later and I'm sure I have at least a concussion, for an older dude Lex can fucking move. He slips my punches like he knows they're coming before I can even think them up. I managed to tag him a few times, but even with that, I have never put him on his ass.

"Pirate, you finished getting your ass beat?" Yang calls out. He's watching us just outside the ring with a smirk on his face. After Lex got here, we'd decided that besides the morning exercises that we get up to do with Archer, boxing was another good way to release some stress. We built a small gym in the compound with a boxing ring and a few other pieces of equipment. Lex out of all of us was the most excited. He'd never get back in the ring again, but at least here he could still train and every once in a while we'd spar with him. He's never lost, but at least we challenge him.

"Yeah, I'm done." I know I am. I was done two rounds ago, but the anger that I felt from earlier still hadn't dissipated. The fighting did nothing. "Thanks Lex."

He nods his head, taking in deep easy breaths, "Anytime."

I remove the boxing gloves, using my teeth to get the first one off and toss it to the ground. I pull the second one and toss it in the same location. "You find anything?" I ask before I can even get close to him.

"Not much. I figured out his name and did a bit of a background check, but he's not too bad. Did some time in juvie. He's a drifter, never lives in one place for very long. His name is Noah Cofield, he's a model, but that's all the big points about him. I got an address if you need it." Yang's eyebrows press in slightly. He has more he wants to say.

"What is it? Just fucking spit it out." I'm not the most patient man right now. Whatever it is, he has to say I just want to hear it so I can move on.

"Have you looked Delia up at all lately? I mean … besides calling to check in on her or bring her in for lockdowns, any background checks?"

"No, why the fuck would I need to do that? I already know who she is. I married her." I don't understand why he would think I would need to go digging that deep into Lia.

"Did you know she was arrested?"

"I don't doubt it with the way her temper is. Why is that a big deal?" I cross my arms over my chest and wait for him to get to the point.

"Well, she was charged, but instead of jail time, they forced her to go to detox. Did you know she was using?"

"Using? Using what?"

"I didn't dig that deep. After detox, they mandated her to go to therapy, anger management. She seems to be trying to get her life on track. I don't know who this Noah guy is, but if he's responsible for helping her, maybe you should let him?" Yang backs up a pace and I'm happy he does. I don't want to strike him, but the way I'm feeling, I just might.

"You're saying that I should just let some other man take care of my Delia, because we're not together?"

"I'm saying maybe it's time you let her go, man. Maybe it's time you start looking for someone you can be with and love the way you love her. It's over between the two of you and she's moved on. It's your turn." Yang twitches one shoulder before he spins on his heel and walks away.

He's the second one today to tell me I need to move on. Even though in my mind I know they're right, I can't. Our relationship was always toxic, but it didn't stop me from loving her. It didn't stop me from wanting to hold her first thing in the morning and last thing at night. The fights and anger didn't stop me from loving her then and won't stop me now. I'm never not going to love Lia, so how the fuck do they expect me to just put that aside and find a new woman to take her spot. No one can take her spot.

Just because I can't be happy doesn't mean that she shouldn't be. If she is truly trying to change and better herself, I couldn't be more proud. If it's this model dude who is helping her do that, he is obviously doing something that I never could. I hate it isn't me who could help her. Except after Yang telling me about the fact that she was in jail and using, it means that there is more to her she hasn't been telling me. I don't know Lia as well as I think I do, but maybe this new guy does.

I need to talk to her at least one last time just to make sure she's okay. If she's with Noah, maybe fucking apologize for being a prick when he was just trying to protect her. Or if I find out that it was indeed him that hit her, then I can beat him down without being in public and embarrassing my club.

Everyone thinks it's time for me to move on and I know deep down that I never will. Even though I know Delia is my forever, I'm man enough to know that she needs to go find whoever is hers. Hippie glasses and all.

CHAPTER

6

Pirate

I TOLD THE BOYS THAT I NEEDED SOME TIME TO THINK. It's true, I used the ride back over here for thinking. Though really I just didn't want to tell them I am rushing back over to find Noah and maybe rip his throat out. If I need the body cleaned up, I'll call them and get in trouble over it later.

Yang was able to get me the boy's address, and it's close to where they were walking. I don't know where she's staying at now, but at least I could find out from him myself if he is the one that put his hands on her. If I believe what he's saying, I can be a man and apologize. If I don't, I can be an asshole and make sure he never puts his hands on another woman again.

I park my bike and walk up the stairs. I bang on the door to his apartment and wait for a second. I stand away from the peephole so he has to open the door to see who it is. I hear him talking and I have to fist my hands inside my pockets to keep myself from swinging the second he opens the door.

"Motherfucker, you got some goddamn nerve!" Noah steps out of the apartment and I pull my hands out of my pockets, ready to fight if that's what he wants to do. I didn't come here for that, but if he wants to throw down, I have more than enough aggression for him.

"Noah, who's there?" The sound of Delia's voice floats through the air and I back up. They're in there together. I didn't think they would be. What the fuck is she doing in his house? I won't fight him with her here. I don't want to hurt her like that.

"Look, man, I'm not here to fight you. Can I talk to Lia please?"

"Fuck you, no." He stands in front of the doorway and crosses his arms over his chest like that's supposed to intimidate me or something like that.

"Kid, I don't know who the fuck you are. But whatever the fuck you think you are going to do to stop me from walking in this damn apartment and seeing her, it isn't going to work. What you need to figure out is if you're ready to get fucked up today?" I take another step forward, almost willing him to swing on me.

"Jimmy? Oh, for fuck's sake." Delia grabs hold of Noah and pulls him back. "What the hell are you doing here? How did you even find me?"

"I have friends."

"Well, why don't you go back to your friends?" She rolls her eyes at me.

I shake my head and squint at her. Delia knows all the Wings of Diablo boys and their women. She may never have lived in the compound with me, but they always treated her like she's family. "They're your friends too, remember."

She stares at me and I wait for her to retort, but she shrugs softly instead. "How's Tink? You guys heard from her?"

"She's good. She's staying with Nitro for now." I relax a bit with talking about Tink. She was missing for months, causing Shyne to almost lose his mind. Now that she's back, it's nice to see him coming back to his normal self.

"Nitro? Who's that?"

"A friend."

"Ya'll just going to shoot the shit in the middle of my fucking hallway? I got neighbors you know." Noah barks out from behind her before he storms off further into the apartment.

"You not going to be a fucking jerk again, are you?" Delia narrows her eyes at me.

"I didn't come here to fight. I came here to ask him a question, but now that you're here I can ask you."

"Fine, whatever." She steps out of the way and I come inside. I glance around and see a few bags with what looks like women's stuff, but the rest of the house looks pretty manly.

"You just moved in?" I ask her.

"Yeah, a few days ago." She answers.

"Congratulations." I grumble without looking at her.

"What did you come here for, Jimmy? I'm tired and want to go to sleep." She says and plops her hands on her hips.

"First and don't lie to me or beat around the bush, all I need is a yes or a no." I glare at her for a second, waiting for her to curse me for forcing an answer out of her. She doesn't like to be forced to do anything. When she only raises her eyebrow and waits for me to continue, I stand there, shocked for a second.

"Yeah, well, did Noah give you that black eye?"

"What the fuck!" Noah barks out. He must be able to hear our conversation from the back room.

"No Jimmy, he didn't do this. Noah would never." She replies, completely ignoring his outburst.

I look around the room and notice the clothes. They look like they are her size. But what is she doing in the living room, wouldn't she move her stuff in the bedroom? "Why don't you got your shit in the room with him?"

She sighs harshly and falls down onto the couch. "Jimmy, I'm trying so fucking hard to not be a vindictive bitch right now, but you're making it too easy. What the fuck does it matter to you?"

"If you say you're trying, then you should know why it fucking matters to me Lia! I don't care where we are in our lives. I'm never not going to want to know you're all right. Yang did some digging into you." She pops up from the couch, and I know she's about to go off. "I didn't tell him to. I told him to look into him. He did it on his own." I put my hands up and back up a step.

She takes in a deep breath and sits back down on the couch. My jaw nearly drops to my chest. She didn't escalate. He must be right about her having to go to anger management. "And what did he find?"

"Well, one thing that you just proved was true. You were in anger management?"

She nods.

"Fuck baby, that's so good. I'm proud of you, truly." I want to reach out and hug her, but I know we're not at that level. Not any more.

"It's nothing to be proud of. I'm not dumb. I knew that if I didn't change, I would have ended up dead or in prison. Getting some sort of zen seemed like a much better option." She sits back on the couch and I gesture with my hand to the seat next to her. When she nods, I take my spot.

"Delia, don't fucking put yourself down like that. Just figuring out that you needed help and going to get it is an enormous accomplishment." I grab hold of her hand and give it a squeeze, but she pulls it away like she doesn't want me to touch her.

"Why aren't you mad?" She cut her eyes to mine.

"Why would I be mad?"

"Because you told me to go to therapy when we were married. You told me constantly that I needed someone to help me with my anger, and all I did was fight you. Now suddenly, I'm all about therapy. I figured you'd be pissed."

I smile for the first time today, "Delia, I don't care how you get the help as long as you get it. It's another reason I came to see Noah. Once Yang told me about some of the shit you'd been going through that I didn't know about, he figured maybe Noah is just the right guy for you. If he's helping you, then you're right about me having no business standing in the way." I lean back against the couch with an emptiness clawing into my gut.

"You are here to give me your blessing?"

"Not my blessing, I'm here to tell you I want you to be happy Lia, even if it's not with me." I give her another smile and she closes her eyes.

"Jimmy, I hate you so much right now." She groans and taps her foot.

"What? Why?" I throw my hands up. I thought I was doing the right thing. I didn't want her to think that I am mad or anything like that.

"You're so damn selfless. I didn't know it before, but that's one reason I was so drawn to you. Always wanting to help others before helping yourself. Honestly, you good with Noah fucking my brains out?" She leans up into my space. When I look into her eyes, I see lust and wickedness playing around in those green orbs.

I grab hold of the back of the couch and bite my tongue. She's baiting me. I know she is. Just like a fucking brat seeing how far she could push my buttons before I lose control. What I don't understand is why she would disrespect her man like this when he's right in the next room. Does she think I wouldn't rail her against the wall, because he might hear me? I would. Fuck how I want to.

"You're telling me you want me coming all over his dick?"

We haven't had sex in years only because I know what would happen if we did—like a junkie trying to take one more hit without becoming addicted again. It's just not possible.

"Delia, stop."

"Fuck that, I'm not going to stop unless you tell me you're okay with that." She hisses in my face.

My chest feels tight. I'm so wound up. Only Delia is ever able to push me to this level. I lean closer and she bites her lip as she stares at me seductively.

The door to the bedroom slams open and I'm instantly on edge. Shit, he must have heard us. He has every right to be pissed.

I watch him grab his coat and beeline for the door, "At least put a sheet down and Delia, remember tomorrow."

A huge gush of air pushes out of her mouth as he walks out of the door leaving me and her there on the couch. That's the weirdest shit I'd ever seen.

"Why did he leave? You two have an open relationship or something?"

"No, you big dummy. Noah and I aren't together. At all, never. And we never will." She drapes her arm over her eyes. "I'm just crashing on his couch for now."

Oh. Thank fuck. I like him more and more now! "What the hell? Why did you put me through all this? Why play all these games?"

"I'm sorry." She whispers, and those two words stop any anger I might have had in its tracks.

"What did he mean by remember tomorrow? He's going to be gone all night?" I lean back, stretch my legs out, getting comfortable.

"No, it's a trick we learned at therapy. That's where I met Noah, if you're going to ask. He's in group therapy with me. Anyway, whenever we feel like we're about to go off the edge or do something impulsive, we have to remember tomorrow. When it comes to anger and impulsiveness, yesterday is easy. Yesterday when I was beating that girl's ass or yesterday when I was smoking that crack I was feeling great, but tomorrow, the day after, is when the world feels like it's going to end. It's always the next day that you are at your worst.

"So, like don't do anything you're going to regret?" I ask, trying to understand what she's saying.

"Sort of. Only I know I don't regret things, but I do have other reasons. Pain, guilt, just wanting to be a better person. Every situation is different." She shrugs.

That's good. "I can appreciate that. Why did he say it just now?"

"He knew I was going to fuck you."

My cock instantly twitches, ready for action. I have to talk myself down. I know damn well we shouldn't be doing that. "Is that his business?"

"Sort of, I'm not in the best of places to be having sex right now." She looks to the other side of the room and rubs her arms.

"Why? Because you're on his couch?"

"No, because …" She turns to me and I can see her eyes are starting to water which puts me on edge immediately. What the hell is going on? "Jimmy, I don't need a cavalry or everything I know you're going to do if I tell you this. It has nothing to do with you. I told the police already, I'm getting over it and I'm okay."

"What the fuck? What's wrong? Why did you have to go to the police? Does it have to do with your black eye?" A million questions fire off in my mind.

"Are you fucking listening Jimmy, because if you're just going to ignore the fucking words that are coming out of my mouth you can leave. I don't need to deal with this shit right now." She snaps at me, but as she does, a tear rolls down her eyes.

"No, okay, I'm listening. I won't do anything. Just tell me what happened,"

"Fine, I was meeting up with a friend of mine. She's still using heavy. I knew I shouldn't have gone, but when I saw her and she invited me, I thought I would hang out for a short while. Maybe get her to come with me to a group session. It was just a little party and I should've left, but I didn't." She's not looking at me anymore. Though my gut and the way she's holding herself lets me know that whatever is coming next is about to make me wish I'd never agreed to letting her handle it her own way.

"Delia, you're scaring the shit out of me." I move closer to her, my hands itching to grab hold of her and pull her close.

"I wasn't fucked up, but everyone else there was. I wound up entertaining a man I shouldn't have and when I was ready to go, he wasn't ready to let me go."

My hand fists and I have to back away from her. "Delia, what are you telling me right now? Are you saying that some limp dick bastard forced himself on you?"

She sighs and squeezes herself tighter. "Yeah, Jimmy, he raped me, okay? I'm damaged goods now, not that I was in prime condition before."

My stomach lurches up into my throat and I have to remember how to breathe. Someone had touched my woman. They'd forced themselves on my Delia. And she wants me to do nothing.

"Jimmy!" she screams at me and I blink a few times, trying to get my eyes to focus. At some point, I must have gotten up and started throwing things around. I don't remember when it happened.

"I'm sorry. I'm sorry. Oh fuck, I'm sorry." I drop in front of her and turn her legs so she is right in front of me. "Delia, who was it? Tell me who or where or what they looked like and I'll make sure ..."

She pushes me back hard. "Dammit, why don't you listen! I don't want you to fix this, Jimmy. I want you to listen! I'm dealing with this. I don't want your entire club pulling people out of their hideaway holes to find someone who is probably too fucking high to remember what the fuck he did. I just want to put it behind me. I want to move on. Honestly, he probably doesn't even realize he raped me."

"What the fuck does that mean? Did you tell him to stop?"

"Of course. I fought and pushed, but you know something is wrong with me, Jimmy. I was ..." She grimaces a little.

I put my hand up and pull her face back to me. "What?"

"I'm weird Jimmy, you know I am. I was turned on, wet. I didn't come, but that's only because he was a quick fuck. I like it rough, I like the pain. He probably didn't know."

"Fuck that, I like a rough fuck too, but when a woman says fucking stop, no matter how goddamn rough that's what it means. Stop." She doesn't respond to me, so I lean up to get in her face, "Lia, look at me. There is nothing wrong with the passion you have for sex, nothing wrong with the way you get turned on, nothing wrong with you."

"There was enough wrong for you to leave." She smirks before she stands up, leaving me kneeling by the couch.

"You know that was different, Lia, it had nothing to do with how you liked to fuck." My mind feels like a fucking tornado with all this information. I can't focus on one thing before I'm jumping to the next. "Wait, is that why you're staying here? Why you're living with Noah?"

"Yeah, I mean, I don't think the guy is coming for me or anything like that, but the doctor said I could have something like PTSD for a while. I keep having night-mares. I don't want to be alone. Noah offered his couch. It hasn't helped any, but at least someone is here to tell me I'm okay."

She's leaning on him to get her through the trauma. No, that's my fucking job. It should be me. "Come live with me. I can protect you and I'll be with you every night. I can— "

"No, absolutely not. You know me. Hell, if Noah didn't say anything before he left, I would have had sex with you. Then you'd be in my nightmares right along with that bastard. I need some time to fucking deal with this. Our marriage was a shit show, because of how I am. I know it. You are one of the last pieces of good I have, don't force me to lose you too."

I feel horrible. I don't want to force her to do anything, but I can't bear feeling this helpless. "I hear you Lia. I want you to know that you're never going to fucking lose me no matter what, but if you want to deal with this on your own, I'm going to support you."

"Thank you, Jimmy." She smiles at me. "I could use my big ol' bear for a nap. If you're not busy?" She says sweetly, just like she used to. I was always much bigger than her, but she used to love curling up halfway on my chest to sleep like a freaking cat. It was annoying, but after almost a year it felt strange any time she wasn't there.

"Sure baby, let's take a nap." I'd be anything she needs me to be right now. I thought with her being away from the club and my life, she would be better protected. Enemies target the wives all the time. She's supposed to be safe. I had let her go so she would find a better life, but I had failed her all at the same time.

CHAPTER 7

Pirate

"NO, STOP. PLEASE!" DELIA WHIMPERS AND I HOLD HER tight until she nuzzles her face into my neck and calms down.

This is the third time she's done this since I've been here. The second time when she clenched on to me, she whispered my name and relaxed against me. I should be happy that she's getting some sleep, but with every nightmare, I get more pissed off. I want to murder someone. I want to hurt whoever did this to her and everyone else they hold dear. Everything in me is saying to disregard what she said about letting the police handle it, but I know if I go against her word, she'll never trust me again. I just can't get my head around sitting here and doing nothing.

I hear the lock on the front door click, and then it opens slowly. Noah must be trying to hear if we're in here having sex.

"You're good." I say to let him know it's cool for him to walk in.

He opens the door all the way, only to see me on the couch with Lia sprawled out halfway on top of me. He doesn't say a word, but I can see the muscles in his jaw twitch. Not sure if he likes my girl or if he just can't stand me. Either way, I'm not about to let whatever petty rivalry we have going on right now keep me from being in Delia's life.

He tries to walk past, but I need to talk to him. "Yo, hold up a minute." I slide myself from under Lia and stay still for a second, just to make sure she doesn't wake up.

"Whatever the fuck you want can wait." He says, backing away from me. For someone who looks so damn soft, he sure is pissed all the time.

"Ease up, I'm not trying to start nothing right now. We both seem to want the same thing. Unless what she told me was wrong. We both want her to be okay." I keep my voice low.

"Yeah, but I'd also like to not get punched in the face. I'm too pretty to be fucking around with you, so step off."

"Too pretty … what the fuck ever, man. Look, I'm man enough to admit that I was fucking wrong. I'm very protective of Delia." I admit.

"Are you? That's strange, because when she was popping those fucking pills, I don't think you were around to protect her. You left her at her worst and you expect me to believe that you want what's best for her? Fuck out of here with that bullshit." He flips me off and tries to walk away.

"Who the fuck do you think you are? You just fucking got here, pretty boy. I was with her when she was at her worst. You think I wanted to leave. You think if I would have known what the fuck she was going through I wouldn't have been at her fucking door every day just to make sure she was straight? I had no fucking choice. We would've killed each other if we stayed together. She would've never gotten the help that she needed. I tried to walk her down that path, but it wasn't something that I could do." I sigh after getting all of that off my chest.

"So what, now you waltz back in looking for a second taste? After you've had your fill of every other woman, you come back to see how she compares?" He crosses his arms over his chest and stares at me.

"Compare? Now I know you don't really know Delia. There is no comparing her. Delia is a fucking goddess. No whore or quick fuck will ever come close to her. I never moved on or replaced her. I've simply been waiting for her to tell me I could come back home." I don't know where it had come from, but even before the words came out of my mouth, I know it's true. Now that she's getting help for her anger, maybe we can try to be with each other again. I've never stopped loving her and now that I can see what being absent from her life has done, I feel like a fucking fool for letting her go.

I LEAVE Delia with Noah after I apologize to him. I believe he'll take care of her, but I need to get my head on straight if I'm really going to get her back. What I need to do is come to grips with what she told me, and I don't know if I can. I'm usually the one the guys come to for advice, but right now I need my brothers. I need someone to fucking guide me, so I don't mess this up.

When I get back to the clubhouse, I see Archer and Jameson at the pool table shooting a round. I guess if there's anyone I could ask about this shit, it'd be them. Jameson had an ex-wife, but she was killed not too long ago and Archer is probably the most level-headed person I've ever met. Together, I'm hoping they can come up with a way for me to cool off.

"Jam, Archer, you two got a few minutes for me?" I say, stopping in front of them.

"Yeah, everything straight? You look more keyed up now than you did before you left." Archer sets the pool cue down and stands tall, looking at me.

"I am, I need … fuck man …" I drag my hands through my hair, trying to find the words to say.

"We're here, brother. You want to go sit?" Jameson walks nearer to me, seeing how close I am to a fucking meltdown.

"Come on, let's go into church." Archer claps me on the back and walks towards the back room where we usually have church.

I follow quietly, trying to push my need to kill someone out of my mind, but it's like a fucking boomerang. Every time I tell myself I can't, the need to do it comes back that much stronger.

Jameson goes to one chair while Archer just sits on the edge of the large wood table itself.

"Now tell us what's up." Archer says.

"Okay, first I know you told me to leave it alone, but I'm a fucking dumb ass and I couldn't. I went over to see that boy Noah."

"Mother fucking hell Pirate! Shit, fine, do we need to call a clean-up crew?" Jameson swears at me.

"No, it's fine. No bloodshed. We want the same things. Turns out Delia was just egging me on. They're not together like that." I tell them, "I wouldn't put it past him if he wanted to get together with her like that, but right now that's not where they are at."

"He told you this?" Archer asks.

"No, Lia did. She lives with him."

"She lives with him, that sounds pretty fucking together to me." Jameson's eyebrows jump up to his hairline.

"It's complicated as fuck, but I believe her. They're in the same therapy group , that's how they know each other."

"Therapy? Shit, that's good news. If there is anyone that needed it, it's Delia." Archer says, nodding his head.

"Yeah, real good." I agree.

"So what's the problem? Everything you've said so far is wonderful." Jameson leans back in his seat.

I close my eyes to get ready for what I'm about to say. Lia told me she didn't want me to call in the calvary, but part of me is hoping that Archer says fuck that we rolling out.

"I'm not even supposed to be telling you this, but I feel like if I don't tell someone I'm going to go out of my mind. She doesn't want me to do anything, and I can't accept just sitting on my hands in my head. My gut feels like something crawled up in there and died. I want to rip someone's fucking throat out. Anyone, everyone, but she won't fucking let me and I can't fucking breathe!" I'm pacing back and forth like a caged animal, and that's exactly what I am.

I fix shit and when I can't fix it, I make sure whoever broke what's mine pays dearly. Lia basically told me someone had tried to break her and is now making me sit here with that knowledge.

"Wait, what? What are you talking about? She doesn't want you to do anything about what?" Jameson shakes his head in confusion.

I take a deep breath and close my eyes. "Someone raped her. That's why she has the black eye, because some asshole forced themself on her." I open my eyes to see the looks of shock on my brother's faces.

"What the fuck!" Jameson stands up from his seat.

"Shit." Archer pushes a hand in his hair.

"She went to the doctors and the fucking police, but she doesn't want us to do anything about it. It's almost like she's blaming herself for what happened. She thinks something is wrong with her." I grit my teeth and do my best to stay still.

"Fuck that, I say we roll out." Jameson looks over at Archer to see what his call is. Now that he's found his woman, he never wants there to be any extra threat. Jameson is always ready to fight, but he's only the VP. Archer's word is law.

"No." Archer answers immediately.

"God dammit! Why not!" I scream at him, no longer able to hold in my frustrations.

"You want to lose her completely?" He captures me in his unwavering gaze.

"No." I'm forced to answer.

"If she trusts you to let her handle this on her own. Let her. You two may not be together, but she's still family. That trauma is hers, Pirate. You need to let her work through this on her own. It'll be hard for you, but imagine how fucked up it is for her. You want to be strong for her, sit with this and help her how she wants to be helped." Archer's words make me want to roll my fucking eyes. Why is he always so logical about shit?

"Speaking of family. I think I want to make her my ol' lady again." I admit to them, but the both of them only share a look, neither say a word.

I look between them, "What?"

"Are you sure you're not just reacting to the news of what happened to her? You weren't there to protect her, so now you're overcompensating." Archer offers.

"Brother, we all know you want what's best for her, but the relationship you had with Delia was border-line toxic. I remember how fucked up it was when you two were still an item. Are you sure you're thinking straight?" Jameson says.

I know they're right, but I can't shake the feeling that this might just be our time. "I hear you and I know what you're saying is right, but she's changing. She's in anger management, she's in recovery, and she's trying hard to better herself. I've changed from where I was years ago, too. I fight harder and to be real with the two of you, I've never stopped loving her. So, if there's a chance …"

"You got to go for it." Archer stands up straight. "I can understand that. If this is what you need to do, I'll support you. Just let us know if you're going to move her in."

I want to, but I'm guessing that it might be a long while before she agrees.

"I'm sorry this shit happened to her. If she needs anything or you do, just let me know. I'm glad you came to us and didn't just run off on your own looking for someone to murder." Jameson gets up from his seat and pulls me into a bro hug.

"I was close, you have no idea."

"I have a little bit of an idea. You remember my woman sacrificing herself, right?" He laughs before he walks by me and out of the room.

"I'll make sure we keep an ear out with local PD to see if they find anything regarding Delia's case. I'll let you know if they do." Archer stands to leave, but I put my hand up to stop him.

"Actually, can I talk to you about one more thing? It's personal." I feel weird asking him about this shit, but if there's anyone here that could help me, it's him.

He leans back against the table and nods for me to continue.

"All right, I realize that this may be too personal so you can tell me to fuck off or whatever. But I'm hoping you could, I don't fucking know, give me a book to read or some pointers, whatever." I mumble in embarrassment.

"Pirate, we're brothers. There's nothing too personal in my life that I won't share with you, besides my woman. Tell me what you need."

"You remember when I said Delia felt like her being raped was her fault?"

"It's bullshit." Archer spits out immediately.

"I know." I agree, "Well she thinks that because she was turned on while he was doing it."

Archer shakes his head, probably getting ready to tell me it's common. Shit I already know. I put my hand up to stop him.

"I know what you're going to say, but this is where I need your help. I know a small bit about your experience, just what the guys joke around about. But Delia thinks she's broken, because she enjoys being hurt while she has sex."

Archer's eyebrows shoot up and a small smirk graces his lips.

"It's going to be awhile before I even think she'll let me be with her like that. But I want to figure out a way to give her what she wants and not push too much. I don't know if I'm even saying this right."

"Are you asking me how to properly dominate Delia?"

"I don't want to hurt her, but I want to please her the way she likes." I tell him.

"What about you? This won't work if you are only doing it for her." He says.

"I like it. I'll be honest with you. I've never been turned on as much as I am with her. Our sex is explosive. But I'm worried that I just lose my head, because she pushes so much. It's like she enjoys getting under my skin."

"She's a brat?" Archer questions.

"What? I mean yeah. I always thought she was. She does shit intentionally to press my buttons, see how far she can push until I lose my shit."

"Okay, then this will work. I can show you the basics, but it'll be uncomfortable for a while. You have a lot to learn."

A lot to learn? If it helps me get my woman back and keep some level of control, then I'll do whatever I have to do.

CHAPTER 8

Pirate

I SPENT THE NEXT FEW DAYS CHECKING ON DELIA AND IT'S surprising how much she truly had changed. Of course, that fire I love is still there just under the surface, but at least now she's not so quick to explode. She does her little meditation and deep breathing techniques, and she de-escalates.

I haven't brought up the fact that I'd like to work on our relationship yet. Though she doesn't seem to hate talking to me when I call. It's a start. I'm just happy she's allowing me to be in her life, even if it's only in this way.

Today I have to make my run over to the casino and check on the winnings. We had a woman take home the progressive jackpot yesterday, so I have to balance everything out.

It feels good to get back to some sort of normalcy now that Rooster is gone.

"Did you see the winner? It was her first time gambling according to her, and she wins the progressive, four million dollars. Talk about fucking beginner's luck." Yang scoffs and packs up the last of the books for me.

"Yeah, tell me about it. I'm happy it was someone in town as well. It'll get the word out that we're up and running again." I close out the books and pack the free cash that we're going to take back to the clubhouse into the security bags that we have for the club.

I walk out of the main area with Yang by my side. He's on the phone with his woman and I have to stop myself from calling Lia. I feel like a fucking school boy. Now that the idea to get back with her had burrowed itself into my head, it's like I can't think about anything else. I don't want to spook her off.

Inside the casino, we have a popular Cajun restaurant that's become a hotspot for many of the couples in town. It's a pleasant surprise since we weren't planning on expanding it, but with all the business it brings in Archer is ready to knock down a wall or two in order to make it bigger.

My eyes scan the crowd waiting to be called to sit, and I see none other than the pretty boy himself. If he's here, then where's Delia? I hope he didn't leave her on her own.

I pat Yang to get his attention before I walk away from him. When we have the cash on our person, we're supposed to stay next to each other. I hear him tell Ice that he'd call her later.

"Noah?" I call over to him. He has his glasses on with a plaid button-up shirt rolled up to his elbows and a fucking trilby hat on. The man is my definition of hipster.

"What?" He answers. The smile he had on his face seconds ago is gone.

"Is Lia here with you?" I get straight to the point.

"What business is that of yours? Last I checked, she was a grown ass fucking woman who could do what the fuck she wants to do when she wants to do it." He turns back to the woman he is with.

I fist my hands at my sides and turn away from him. I've been fucking trying with him on the sole strength that Lia cares for him, but I don't take anyone talking to me like that.

"What the fuck is that about? Who's he?" Yang asks.

"That's Delia's roommate." I say through gritted teeth.

"Oh shit, the one I dug up all that information about? Well shit, I'm with you if you still want to fuck him up. He's acting like a fucking asshole." Yang says.

"I can't, Lia would have a full on meltdown if something happens to him." I reply.

We make it outside to the truck we use for pickups and I get in behind the wheel. I should just go on about my business, but I hate the fact that I don't know who's with Lia. I don't want to call her just for her to give me her location, but at the same time, not knowing she's okay is driving me up the fucking wall.

"You want to go back in or what?" Yang asks leaning back in his seat.

"Yeah, you going to be good for—" Just as I'm about to jump out of the car, the exit opens and I see Noah walking out. He's pissed. I can almost see the anger coming off his body in waves.

"Ain't that him right there?" Yang sits up in his seat.

I nod, but don't get out of the truck.

The door opens again and five more people come outside. Most people use the front or the back entrance to get in and out of the casino. This one, since it only leads to a small parking lot used mostly by the workers, is usually not so busy.

"I told you I'm not just letting my fucking money train go. You think you just going to ignore my fucking calls and that's the end of it?" One man is wearing a black polo shirt and dark jeans, and his hair is combed back.

His face looks like he took a bath in grease and he has a bit of a limp to him.

"And I fucking told you I'm not doing that shit. I paid you, that is the end of it."

I can hear Noah through my window. I don't know what he's into, but this shit isn't happening.

"We need to handle this?" Yang asks with his hand on the door, ready to jump out if I tell him too.

"Let me see what he does. If they swing on him, we help him out." He may be an asshole to me, but Delia trusts him. I want to see what kind of person he is. If he's doing shady shit, I don't want her around him.

"You don't really have a choice, now do you? Your sister is doing her part. Why don't you do yours? You lived good off my shit for years, it's time to pay up."

Noah steps into the main guy's face and the four other men that came outside surround him. This shit is getting bad and fast.

"I never touched your shit. You're looking for my fucking mother. You can take up any problems you have with her. Until then, stay the fuck away from me."

I have to strain to hear what Noah is saying.

"You don't want to pay? Fine, we can get this month's payment a different way." One man to the side lunges for him, wrapping his arms around Noah's neck.

"Shit, let's move." I tell Yang and we both rush out of the truck.

The group of them toss Noah down on the ground and stomp on him. I can't allow that. Even if I didn't know him, he's on our property.

I grab hold of one man and fling him off Noah. I swing my fist into the face of another one. Yang wrestles with another of them and Noah is pushing his way up from the floor. He jumps up, ready to fight. He cocks his fist back, ready to swing in my direction until he sees it's me and I'm trying to help him.

He quickly turns and swings at one of the other men that were trying to jump him. The three of us make it a fair game and it's not long before the five men that were just trying to jump Noah are all on the ground, bleeding from different parts of their bodies.

The man that was doing all the talking addresses Noah.

"You fucked up boy. Wait until Mad Jack hears about this. You think he came for you before, you going to wish you just gave us the fucking money." The man on the ground laughs and I step in front of Noah, leaning down so the man on the ground can see my face.

"I don't know who the fuck Mad Jack is or what the hell he has to do with Noah, but whatever business that needs to be taken care of know that the Wings of Diablo will be right behind him to make sure that this shit doesn't happen again."

"The Wings of Diablo?" The man on the floor scoffs, "Oh, we know about you. I'm not sure you want to get mixed up in this. It's bad for your health."

"You keep fucking talking to us like that. This conversation is going to be bad for your health." Yang growls out from behind me.

I don't say anything else. I turn and grab Noah by his shoulder to turn him around towards the truck. He keeps his shoulders back and his head high, but I can see he's having a hard time taking in a deep breath. His ribs must be fucked up.

"You good?" I ask him, but keep my voice low so the people behind me don't hear us.

"I'm fine. You didn't have to help me." He grunts out.

"You don't have to help Delia, but you do. You do right by her. That means you are all right by me. I'm not just going to stand by and let you get your ass kicked." I huff out a low laugh.

"I could have taken them." Noah says.

"Taken them where? To dinner? Because you sure as hell wasn't about to win that fight." Yang says as we get in the truck.

"Whatever, man." Noah slides into the back seat of the van and basically collapses.

"You sure you good? You need a medic?" I turn to him.

"Nah, I just need to get fucking home. I've had worse than this." Noah says through gritted teeth. "She went to therapy. Mondays and Fridays she has therapy. Every other Wednesday is the group session." He tells me with his eyes closed.

"Thanks." I say, but leave it at that. He clearly needs some rest. "I'll get you home."

I DROP Yang off with the cash at the clubhouse, but stay true to my word and help Noah get home.

I want to know more about what kind of shit Noah is running away from, but right now isn't the time. As long as he's not bringing that shit around Delia, I'll leave it to him to let us know what's going on.

He gives me his key to get into the apartment. I walk in to see Delia sitting on the couch with a bowl of popcorn in her lap and a pair of pajamas on.

"What the fuck! Jimmy, what the hell did you do?" She yells and rushes off the couch, completely forgetting about the snack in her lap.

"I didn't do this. I'm just bringing him back." I don't know how much she knows about what's going on with him, but it's his problem to tell her about.

"He helped me." Noah wheezes out.

"Noah, don't be a fucking macho man. Do you need a doctor?"

"No man, I'm good. I just want to go lay down. Delia, you okay?" He asks her.

She rings her hands, but doesn't reach out for him. "Yeah. I'm fine. Nothing life altering in therapy today."

"All right, wake me if you need to talk." He says and walks off slowly to his bedroom room.

"What the fuck happened?" She puts her hands on her hips and stares at me.

"I don't know what was going on. He was at the casino and had a beef with a few dudes. Yang and I helped him out, and I brought him back here." I shrug, not wanting to let her know he was being threatened.

"Thanks, I really appreciate you helping him."

"Of course." I reply, but I'm not paying attention to what she's saying anymore. I'm looking at her body. She's wearing cartoon pajama pants and a plain black V-neck t-shirt. She has a pair of furry slippers on and her hair is piled up on top of her head. Her outfit isn't revealing or form fitting, but it's still sexy as fuck to me.

What I would give to be balls deep inside of her right now.

My cock gets hard at the thought and I don't even bother to hide it from her. I want her to know how much I want her.

"Is that for me?" She asks, tilting her head to the side.

"It sure as fuck isn't for Noah." I reply.

"Is that why you helped him? You want a quick fuck?" She squints at me.

"No. I helped him, because he needed help." I keep my answer clear.

"Hmm, I think you have an ulterior motive, Jimmy. Is that what this is? I was wondering why suddenly you were so interested in keeping in contact with me. You want to fuck the used and abused girl? My pussy is still tight even after—"

I turn before she can finish her sentence and walk to the door.

"Hey, where the fuck are you going! Don't turn your back on me." She runs up behind me and grabs hold of my arm to turn me around.

I've been talking with Archer a lot over the past few days and it turns out that this type of behavior is normal in brat subs, according to him. They want to submit, but they want the person they submit to, to prove they are worthy. Just giving them what they want isn't the way. I can't fuck her today, even if she's ready to let me.

Right now, Delia wants me to blow up, but I'm not going to.

"Lia, I will not stay here and listen to you talk about yourself like that." I keep my voice low, sweet-like.

Her eyebrows dip slightly. "It's the truth. I'm damaged."

"You're not damaged and until you realize that to be true, nothing will happen between us. No matter how badly I want it to." I grab hold of my cock and re-adjust myself. I'm going to need a cold shower to get this erection to go down.

"What do you mean? Why are you playing with me? We're over, remember? Nothing is going to happen between us." She looks up at me.

"Delia, just because papers went to some judge that said we were over doesn't mean it's true. I'm not over you. I love you still, every part of you. I had thought because we were so different it meant we weren't supposed to be together. But now I see it was just the wrong time. I don't know how you feel about me, but I know that I'm never going to want anyone the way I want you."

Her shoulders drop slightly, "You want me? You love me?" She asks like she isn't sure she heard me right.

"Fuck yes, I love you Delia. I know the both of us are different now, but I think that will make what we have that much stronger." I move a little closer, fighting with myself about my decision not to fuck her brains out. "Even if you don't want the same things I do, I promise you I'm not going anywhere. But I'm willing to bet that you feel this connection we still have the same way I do. I think you still feel that pull deep inside for me the way I feel it for you. I've never stopped thinking about how fucking good the good times were when we were together, Lia. How insane you make me and how much I fucking want that again. Do you feel it, Lia?" I lean down closer to her, my lips only a breath away from hers.

"I do. I feel it." She raises her hands to touch me, but I back away. Her bottom lip pokes out. "You said you wanted …"

"I want you, but I also said nothing is going to happen until you get this fucked up notion out of your head that you're damaged."

"You won't be able to hold out." She says with a smirk on her face.

"We'll see." I shrug and walk out with my raging hard on and Delia breathing heavily leaning against the wall.

CHAPTER

9

Delia

NOAH AND I PULL UP AT THE WINGS OF DIABLO clubhouse for a family party. Jimmy always said I was part of the family, but I've never really felt that way. I've always been the crazy ex-wife. Things have really been different over the past month since Noah and I had run into Jimmy on the street.

It's been two weeks since Jimmy admitted to me he wanted to give our relationship another chance and that he's still in love with me. He still desires me, but true to his word, we've done nothing.

I'm going out of my mind.

"This shit is cool as fuck. They all live here?" Noah asks. It took a few days, but he and Jimmy have developed a bit of a bromance. It's nauseating. Jimmy actually came over to my house the other day to watch the fucking game with him instead of being with me. I hated that I loved it so much.

"Yeah, it's like one big fraternity except it's a bunch of bikers." I shrug and we walk inside to a man being held upside down with a fucking funnel in his mouth.

"Well fuck, you weren't playing." Noah barks out in laughter.

I didn't expect to be this on point. Jimmy sees me walk in and rushes over to me. I don't know if it's him that's changed or me, but things are so different this time around. I will say he is trying much harder than he ever did. He buys me flowers and stops by just to check on me. He's patient with me when I fly off the handle, but most of all, he makes sure that I'm kind to myself.

I know the road back from the type of assault that I endured is going to be long, but everyday he makes me feel more and more like myself.

He wraps me up in a huge bear hug and lifts me off the ground to kiss me swiftly before putting me down. "Hey, why didn't you let me know you were close? I would have met you guys outside and walked you in." He's all smiles.

"I'm a big girl Jimmy, one little door isn't going to stop me. What I want to know is what the hell you guys are doing in here?" I point over his shoulder.

"Oh, you know we have to act a fool, our brother's home." Jimmy smiles so brightly and I can see the happiness in his eyes. When we were married, he tried to explain to me what it felt like to be a part of a brotherhood, both in the military and with the motorcycle club, but I didn't understand. Now that I've found Noah, I get it, at least to an extent. Family isn't necessarily the people of your blood, sometimes it's the people that choose to be in your life no matter what.

Today's celebration is to welcome Shyne back home. He was gone for a while to find his cousin Tink. Only now that she's back safe and sound, Shyne has come back too.

"I'm surprised there aren't strippers hanging from the rafters." I tease.

"Strippers? Rafters? Where do I sign up for that party?" Noah says and walks further in, leaving Jimmy and I alone.

Jimmy turns away from me for a second and calls for Archer. When he gets the man's attention, he points to Noah, who is walking around like he owns the place, and Archer nods in silent approval.

"Wouldn't want you to get in trouble." I poke fun at him.

"It's not about getting in trouble Lia, it's about respect." He replies.

"Hey Delia, how are you doing?" Daria, Archer's woman, comes up next to me and gives me a hug.

She's always nice to me, but then again, Daria is about the most submissive person I've ever met in my life. I'm sure if I slapped her face, she'd forgive me for it without so much as an argument.

"I'm much better. Seems like everyone is having a good time." I gesture to the bar where Shyne is already stumbling and laughing.

"Yeah, we're all so happy Shyne is back home. It wasn't the same without him." She smiles and walks off to talk to someone else.

Another woman comes over to Jimmy and drapes her arm around his midsection, giving him a slight hug before she waves at me and walks off.

She's gorgeous and I feel a cold stab of jealousy deep in my gut. "Looks like you have plenty to keep you occupied." I shove my hands in my back pockets and bite the inside of my mouth.

"What?" Jimmy turns in my direction.

"I'm just saying. I don't know what you brought me here for when you have women like that already here for you." I point to the girl that just walked off.

"Are you fucking serious?" He squints at me and I feel the anger inside of me building up.

"You want to see how fucking serious I am?" I scream at him.

I wait for him to scream back, but he just stares at me until he softly says, "Go upstairs into my room and take your clothes off. If you whisper even one more word, I'll make sure you don't come tonight."

My mouth drops open and I'm stuck between wanting to scream at him, but also wanting him to make me come. It's been so fucking long.

I know he means what he says, especially since he'd stayed true to his word about nothing happening until I accepted the fact that I'm not damaged.

I slam my mouth shut and do what he says. Quietly, I walk up the stairs and into his room. I take my clothes off and wait for him to walk in. Though after fifteen minutes, he still hasn't shown up and I'm getting pissed off again.

I wait another five minutes and just as I'm about to put my clothes on to go back downstairs; he walks in.

"It's about fucking time." I get into his face, but before I can raise my hand, he grabs hold of my cheeks and squeezes them hard enough to get me to stop talking.

"Delia, we're not going to do it that way this time around. I will not permit you to talk to me just anyway you want to talk to me. You're not going to put your hands on me in an aggressive way or I promise you will not like what I do to you."

That minor threat coming from him is enough to put me on edge. The fact that he's so calm about it is throwing me off. Is he mad? Is he calling us off? Are we going to have sex? What is happening here?

"You're not going to do anything to me." I say, but instead of the firm voice I thought would come out, all I hear is a small whisper.

He smiles and walks over to his closet. "Lia, what do you want? Tell me."

"I don't want anything." I deny.

"No? Okay. I want something. Will you give it to me?" He pulls out a large gym bag.

"What's in it for me?" I ask.

"You'll come as many times as you want, and I'll fuck you as hard as you can take." He says without looking at me.

"That sounds like a good deal. What do you want?" I say.

"Lie down," He orders. He pulls out a pair of hand-cuffs and it feels like I'm going to soak through the sheet on the bed.

"What are you going to do?" I ask him, but there's no answer. Instead of waiting for him to respond, I simply do as he asks and lie down.

"Can I tie you down? I'll take care of you. You're safe here. I'm never going to let anything bad happen to you. Do you trust me?" He asks me, showing me the cuffs and I nod my head. He gently pushes a strand of hair out of my face before he presses his lips to mine and kisses me deeply.

"Good girl. Get comfortable." He tells me and suddenly all I want is for him to say it again. I relax my arms and wait for him to put me in the position that he wants. He cuffs my arms and my ankles to his bed frame, leaving me completely spread eagle.

He pulls a pink and strangely shaped tadpole looking apparatus out of the bag next. He brings it up to my face to show it to me. "How about this, my sweet princess? Can we play with this?"

Did he just call me his princess? Why the fuck do I like this so much?

"What's that?" I ask, my voice sounds like a breathy whisper.

"Just a toy, for fun." He pulls out something that looks like a small remote and presses a button, which activates the small pink toy. It instantly starts vibrating and I flinch in surprise.

"You're so fucking sexy Lia. God, I don't know how I've gone so long without you. I feel like I'm dying inside." He bends down and kisses me hard again. He slides his lips to my jaw and down my neck, leaving a trail of wet kisses behind.

"So fuck me Jimmy. I want you too." I whine and feel him smirk against my neck.

"I know. I know your body almost better than I know my own." He drags the vibrating toy down the trail he just left with his mouth and goosebumps erupt over my entire body. My back arches up as he leans down and sucks on my nipple before rolling the vibrator over it. I feel him grinding himself down onto the bed and I can see how turned on he is. I want him now.

"You always smell so good, mouthwatering." He kisses down my stomach until he reaches my slit, and then he softly licks up my sensitive area. My body convulses with pleasure rushing through my body.

"Jimmy, now. I can't take this anymore. I need you inside of me." I pull on the restraints and notice that while they hold me secure, they aren't biting into my arms. It's not painful.

"I know how much you can take, sweetheart. You're stronger than you give yourself credit for. You're stronger than any other woman I've ever met."

I feel a blush creeping up my neck and onto my face. I don't feel strong, but to hear that he thinks that about me makes me feel good on the inside.

He leans back down and continues to lightly lick and suck on my clit. My stomach hurts from how much I'm clenching it. It's like the sweetest, slowest torture I've ever gone through in my life.

I feel the small vibrator pressing against my pussy lips before he lifts his head and looks me in the eye. "Do you trust me, baby? Can you take this for me?"

"Yes, I can do it for you." I reply, wanting to do whatever he wants.

"You can do anything, including drive me absolutely wild. There'll never be another woman like you." He murmurs as he presses the small toy inside of me and turns the vibration up a little. I'm going to come so fast using this. Maybe that's the plan. He did say he was going to make me come.

"Oh Jimmy, I'm close. More." I tell him, but instead of turning it up, he turns it down. "No!" I complain.

He stands and moves farther away from me. I turn my gaze on him, trying to figure out what he's doing. "Delia, do you trust me?" He crosses his arms over his chest. He's upset.

"What, we are going to talk about this now?" I pull at the restraints and he turns the vibrator up in my pussy so high that my eyes roll in the back of my head and I stop breathing for a second. He turns it back down and stares at me.

"I asked you a question." His voice is soft, but his gaze is intense and almost scary.

"Yes, I trust you Jimmy. You know I do."

"Good, then you're going to have to trust me fully now. You need to learn that there is some shit that you just can't do to me anymore. Causing a scene where one isn't warranted like you did downstairs is one of them. When you do things I don't like, I'm going to punish you."

I scoff and shake my head at him. "Punish me? You can't punish me." The vibrator deep inside me goes off again and my body jerks off the bed. He pushes me right to the edge and then backs off.

"Oh shit, Jimmy. Please. I'm sorry! I won't do it again." I say just so I can come. I'd speak a different language if it means he'd leave the fucking vibrator on.

"No baby girl. We both know you're only saying that right now, but by the time I'm finished with you tonight you're going to mean it. You're going to know that if you try to do this again, how much it's going to hurt and how disappointed you make me." He comes back over to me, caresses my hair and looks me deep in my eyes.

His eyes are full of hurt, and I just want to wipe it away. "I didn't mean to disappoint you. I'm sorry."

He leans down to kiss me and I lean up as much as I can to deepen the kiss. He has to pull himself away, "You're in punishment right now only for what you did downstairs, but if you keep on tempting me like this, it'll last a lot longer than I plan on making it." He kisses my forehead and I lean back against the bed.

"What the hell are you talking about? What is going to last a lot longer?" Now I'm fucking confused.

"If you cause a scene or scream, I'll stop and send you home like this. If you're a good girl and take your punishment as I see fit, then before the night is over I promise I'll be deep inside of you if you want me."

"Yes! That's what I want, so come do it!" I snap at him and he raises the vibration again before he lets it drop to a barely notable level.

"Be good for me." He says before he turns on his heel and walks out. The motherfucker walked out of the room and left me tied up to the bed like a goddamn prisoner or something. I don't know what the fuck he thinks he's doing, but I'm not with it. If I wanted to be in jail, I would have—

The vibration on the small toy inside my pussy increases and my walls clamp down on it. He can control it from wherever he is in the clubhouse? I try to get some friction, but I can't close my legs, because of how he'd trussed me up. The vibrations go away, but my need to come only intensifies.

"Oh shit! No!" I complain and try to pull against the restraints again. I can't get out.

When I get out of here, I'm going to give him a piece of my mind. He can't treat me this way. I didn't do anything wrong. So what if I had a brief outburst? I always have outbursts. He knows that's how I am. He said that he loved me, "Oh … fuck." The vibration ramps back up and I bear down again, trying to finish the wave, but he leaves me hanging right at the very end of it.

"No!" I scream before I clamp my mouth shut. He said if I screamed, he'd make me go home like this—wanting. Does that mean he's not going to let me come? Fuck, I can't scream. I can hold it in. I'm sure of it.

My thighs shake from the intense need to close them, but I can't. I don't know when he had learned any of this stuff, but he wasn't into playing around like this when we were married. Hell, I hadn't even known I was into playing with all this stuff until tonight.

Over and over like clockwork Jimmy tortures me until I'm laying on the bed crying my eyes out. I call for him, but he doesn't come. Part of me thinks of just screaming my head off to get out of here, but I tell myself that if I give up I won't get my prize. I hate to lose. If I'm honest with myself, I think I'm more worried about disappointing Jimmy than I am about winning.

The door opens and Jimmy walks back in with a bottle of beer in his hands.

"I'm … I'm sss ... sorry!" I cry.

"Oh baby girl, I know you're sorry. You're a good girl. I know you didn't mean to hurt me, but you did. That woman you were jealous of downstairs, do you remember?"

I think back to what got me into this mess. I was mad that the pretty girl had hugged him. I'll admit now it wasn't anything crazy, just a hand around the waist, and she even acknowledged that I was there before she walked off. I didn't need to get so upset. I see that now. "Yes, I remember. I shouldn't have yelled. She didn't do anything."

"No, she didn't. She's family. That's Bones' ol' lady. She'd never cheat on him with me or anyone else in the club-house, and I'd never cheat on you. Now that we're trying to get us back on track, there's no one else I'm thinking about other than you and the fact that you don't see that hurts me." He explains himself and I hear every word. He didn't have to scream. We didn't have to fight and there's no bloodshed, but I am about to go out of my mind.

"I'm sorry. I see that. I know you won't cheat on me. I was insecure. She's so pretty, and she touched you. I wanted to touch you." I admit, letting my true feelings come tumbling out of my mouth.

"Oh baby, I want to touch you, too. I want to fucking destroy you before I help you pick up the pieces and put them back together again." He rubs a hand over his pants.

"I want that. I'll be good. I won't do that again. Please, just let me out of here and fuck me. I can't take this." I whimper and pull at my restraints again.

"You can take it, my sweet girl. I promise I'll never do more than you can take, but seeing you tied up like that. So beautiful, so fucking perfect, it's more than I can take." He pulls his pants down and I see his long cock as he yanks it out of his boxers.

My mouth waters and I lean forward as much as I can, but it's not very far. "You want to do this?" he asks, his voice husky with his hand wrapped around his cock. The muscles in his arms are tensed up.

"Yes, God yes."I hiss out and try to move again even though I already know that I'm not going to be able to get anywhere.

He walks over to where I am laying and he lets his cock hover just far enough away from my mouth that I can't taste him.

"Delia, if you hurt me, same deal. You want me to reward you, don't you?" He strokes his cock slowly and I mewl at the sight. I never thought I'd want to be good for anyone, but I'd do anything right now to be his good girl.

"Please, Jimmy." I lick my lips, knowing that I would never intentionally hurt him like that. At least not now.

"I'm here Lia. I'm always going to be here for you." He presses the crown of his cock against my lips and I open up for him. I suck him in as hard as I can and he groans loudly.

"Fuck, oh fuck!" He pulls out of my mouth and lifts his cock for a second before he lets it go and slides back into my mouth. I use my neck muscles to help me bob up and down on his length, all the while he praises me and tells me how good I make him feel. He turns the vibrator on, not at its max speed, but faster than it was a second ago, while he grabs my head and pushes himself deep down my throat.

"I'm going to fuck your throat, Lia. It's going to be hard. Can you take it?"

I can't talk, but I nod my head. He does exactly what he'd said he was going to do. Slamming his dick down my throat hard enough to have me gagging and mucus coming out of my nose. I try to keep up, but he's relentless. I rip my mouth away, but he grabs my hair and turns my face back to him.

"Open!" he barks at me and I respond immediately. He fucks my throat for a few minutes longer and the pressure in my core builds to an unbearable level.

I scream with tears and snot trailing down my face begging for whoever is listening to just let me come this one time, but just when I think I may fall off the edge he turns the toy off and yanks himself out of my mouth. His dick is red and angry looking. He hasn't come either.

"No! Oh Jimmy, please … Please. I fucking learned my lesson. It's too much!" I beg him.

"Don't cry baby. I'm here." He pushes his rock hard dick back into his boxers and lifts his pants. He grabs a napkin and wipes my face off. He checks my wrists and my ankles before he leans down and kisses me hard again. "Who are you to me?"

"Your ex-wife. Your girlfriend." I say, trying to figure out what the right answer is. If it would get him to give me what I want, I'd tell him I'm a fucking Chihuahua.

"Be good, baby." He says and walks out of the room, leaving me literally crawling out of my skin with the need to orgasm.

Again another round of teasing me. Getting me right to the edge and denying me. More tears and more begging.

I don't know how long I've been trussed up like this, but it feels like hours. Yet every time he opens the door I can hear everyone down stairs still partying.

The fourth time he comes in, I'm at my limit. I'm ready to give up. I don't want to win anymore. I don't want a prize. I just want to stop. I want him to hold me.

"Who are you to me, Lia?"

I think about the question this time instead of just saying the first things that come to my mind. I turn it around and ask myself what Jimmy is to me.

He was one of the main reasons I'd agreed to go to therapy. He's the good in my life I feel I don't deserve. He protects me even when I intentionally make things hard for him. He loved me when I was at my worst. He accepted me when I did nothing but try to tear him down. Even now, when our future is unclear he commits himself to me in a way that I know no matter what he's always going to be there. Married, fuck buddies, enemies, or whatever, he's always going to be there just like he always is. He's my everything.

"I'm everything. I'm your everything." I say, looking into his eyes. His shoulders drop and he lets the remote fall from his hand.

"Yes, Delia, you're my everything." His voice is thick with emotion. He makes quick work of undoing the straps that hold my legs before he softly pulls the toy out of my pussy, that one sweep against my insides is enough to have me whimpering in need.

"I need you." I tell him and raise my hands to wrap them around his neck the second he releases them.

"You have me. You've always fucking had me." He tugs his shirt over his head and flings it to the floor. He spreads my legs wider. The rough material of his jeans scratching against my already overly sensitive thighs has me panting with need. I want him to hurry, but if there's anything I've learned in our brief session here tonight it's that I'm not in control of this. There is nothing I can say that's going to force him to react how I want him to react, and surprisingly, I'm more than okay with that.

CHAPTER 10

Pirate

LIA'S ENTIRE BODY IS SHAKING, BUT THIS IS THE MOST docile I've ever seen her. Who'd have thought a little denial was all I needed to do to get her to stop acting crazy. I laugh internally, because even I'm not stupid enough to think that this was all me.

I want to take my time, but I'm so wound up I know that it's not going to happen. I kick my pants off and notch the head of my dick against her swollen folds. My girl likes it rough, but she'd gone through an ordeal a few weeks ago. I never want to be in the same category as the bastard that forced himself on her. This part of the night, I need her to know just how in charge she is.

"Lia, baby girl, I want to hurt you. But I don't want to push it too far. You control this. If you want me to stop, you say it and I'm off of you."

"I never want you to stop, please give it to me." She hooks her leg over my ass and tries to pull me in.

A deep angry rumbling growl settles in my chest, "Don't make me punish you again." I warn her and she instantly stops what she's doing. "I don't want to fuck this up. If tomorrow morning I wake up and find out that you let me hurt you too bad, I'll never fucking trust you again."

She needs to realize just how much we need trust in this relationship for this level of intensity to exist. I want to do all the fucked up things to her body she wants me to do, but I don't want her permanently hurt, mentally or physically.

"I hear you Jimmy. I promise. If it's too much, I'll tell you to stop." She nods her head and I push forward into her cunt.

It feels like I've died and gone to heaven. So fucking good.

Before I came back up here, I went to the bathroom and jacked one out. There's no way I was going to last if I didn't. It was the most unsatisfying orgasm I've ever had in my life.

Her walls instantly start pulsating slowly, letting me know she is right on the edge of coming. She deserves it. She deserves to feel good. I thrust in as deep as I can go and she wails out at the intrusion.

I grab hold of her hair and yank her head to the side so she can't move again. Her nails dig into my skin and I buck into her like an animal.

"Oh God, oh God, oh God ..." She sucks in a huge breath before she comes hard and fast on my dick. The feel of her walls clamping down on me only spur me to go harder.

"Yes, Lia. Fuck, that's it." I press her leg up against her chest and slam into her. There's no way she's not going to be sore tomorrow.

I pull out of her and flip her over so she's laying on her stomach. I pull her knees back so her ass is up in the air. I slam into her and as I thrust inside I smack her ass hard and pull her head back using her hair.

"Oh, fuck I love it." She squeals and bucks back against me. She is soaking wet, her body is still trembling from the first orgasm she just had, but I have so much more in store for her. I reach around her waist and flick my finger against her clit, causing her to freeze up and forget to move.

"No, you don't, keep fucking me." I pull her head up and bite down on her neck. She cries out and continues meeting me thrust for thrust.

She comes again and falls down to the bed, her body's already exhausted from her denial session earlier and the two orgasms she's just had. She heaves in deep breaths, but I'm not done with her.

I turn her over to her back again and squeeze her breast hard enough to hurt. She hisses and juts her foot out. It connects with my gut, but not as hard as I know she can kick. She falls down to the floor and crawls backwards slowly.

"Are you running from me, sweet girl? That's just going to make me angry." I climb out of the bed and slowly walk in her direction.

"Yeah? And what happens if you get angry? If I'm bad, will it hurt?" She asks, her voice low and taunting.

"Keep it up and find out, fucking brat." I swear at her.

I don't see anger on her face. I see mischievousness. She likes this game. "Get back over here, don't make me have to drag you off the fucking floor." I stalk toward her like a predator going after my prey. Suddenly, she turns and tries to crawl out the door. I grab hold of her leg and drag her back. She turns and smacks me hard across the face again. Nowhere near as hard as she can, these are Lia's versions of love taps. She's still playing with me. I pin her hands down, getting myself between her legs to spear myself into her.

She screams out and groans with each hard thrust. I let go of her so I can grip her back and shoulders for more leverage. She digs her nails into my arms and pulls down, leaving what I'm sure will be deep scratches. I rear back from the pain, but she follows me, throwing my body off balance. We fall back down to the ground with a heavy thud, but it doesn't stop us from going at it.

She readjusts her legs and slides down on my cock. The sight is almost more than I can take. I want to make this last so much longer, but I don't have the willpower or the self-restraint to hold back. Besides, I know there is much more to come after this. I don't need much down time and as long as she wants me, I will take all I want from her tonight.

She rocks her core against me and my hands curl into the curve of her hips. I drink in large gulps of air as my body urgently races to its own release.

"Perfect." I mutter just as the muscles in the small of my back twinge and my abs contract.

"I love you, Jimmy." She whimpers as she lets her head fall back and comes yet again with me deep inside of her.

I grasp her ass and squeeze as I slam her down one last time on my dick. A light, buzzing numb feeling rolls through my body as euphoria seizes and erases every thought I've ever fucking had.

How the fuck could I ever think I could move on from Delia. Her passion is my passion. There's no moving on from someone like Delia. She's it for me and I'm happy I'm getting a second chance to show her.

I WAKE up in the middle of the night to see Delia snuggled up close in my arms. My heart feels like it's going to explode out of my chest. I'm so happy. The few tips Archer had given me worked like a charm. I'm going to have to sit with him again and see what else he could teach me.

Not only did the faux punishment push her to a new height, but it added to our lovemaking. It lets me know she trusts me enough to take her to that level and that she truly doesn't want to hurt me with shit that comes out of her mouth.

Sure, we still fuck hard and I'm sure shit is going to be hurting tomorrow, but it feels way more controlled now than it's ever been. It feels like we've got a whole new lease on life together and I can't wait to see what happens next.

"Are you going to tell me what's got you smiling like the cat who ate the canary?" Lia mumbles as she stretches and looks up at me.

"You. I got you back. I feel like a fucking champion over here." I lean down and kiss her softly.

"I'm not much of a prize." She shakes her head.

I stare at her for a second, not saying a word, and just glare at her.

"Okay, sorry. I'm feeling like you fought well for me." She snuggles further into my arms.

"Are you hurting? Do you need anything?" I shift in case she needs me to get up and find something for her.

"Yes, I'm hurting, but it's so good. I haven't felt a hurt like this in years. I must have forgotten what completely satisfied felt like."

"I can promise you'll never forget again." I drawl.

"We're really doing this, huh?" She chuckles.

"Did you think I was playing?"

"No, not playing. But I was sure that I'd fuck it up, or you'd remember just how horrible we were before or I'd realize the man I built up in my head wasn't nearly as great as I was making you out to be. I just figured something would go wrong by now."

She'd built me up in her head. I'm not sure what the fuck I did to get a woman like her, but I'm going to thank my lucky stars every night. "Am I as great as you made me out to be?" I ask her, staring into those sapphire blue eyes that I'd already lost myself in once before.

"You're better, so much better." She leans up and kisses me.

Everything is exactly how I envisioned it would be, except one thing.

"Delia, move in with me."

She blinks and laughs after a second. "Wait, you're serious?"

"Fuck yeah, I'm serious. I don't want to be without you anymore, not even one fucking night. Come live with me." The words flow out of my mouth without hesitation.

"Oh, Jimmy." She grabs hold of my face, "No."

I pull away from her, my feelings more than a little hurt. "What? Why not? I thought shit was going good here."

"It is. It's going great. But we just got together." She sits up in bed.

"No, we just got back together. What do we need a fucking preliminary period for? We know everything about each other. I'm not understanding the fucking hold up." I try to keep the anger out of my voice, because I know that's a fucking trigger for her.

She stops talking and just sits there breathing. Already different from who she was before. "Jimmy, we don't know everything about each other. Who I was five years ago isn't who I am now. Sure you may know some of my tricks from days past, but you don't know me."

I huff out a quick breath and sit up myself, only to have her climb on my lap and hold my face.

"I want us to work, Jimmy. More than anything besides my sobriety, but I need to take things slow."

I grimace before I wrap my hands around her small waist. "Take things slow. What does that mean? Like no fucking?"

"No fucking? What? No, plenty of fucking. All the fucking. Fucking all the days." Lia says enthusiastically, causing me to laugh.

"Then tell me what slow means?" I compose myself so I can hear her conditions.

"We get to know each other, stay honest, and take this one day at a time. We don't need to run back to where we were just because this is all familiar ground. I want to know shit about you I missed out on when all I could think about was how to piss you off."

"Fuck, that sounds like dates and shit." I fall back and drape my arm over my eyes. It's been years since I'd gone on a date, let alone one I had to think up.

She moves my arm so she can look me in the eye. "Yeah, I expect to be wined and dined. I'm older now, my taste is way more expensive than it used to be." She waggles her eyebrows and I groan in defeat.

CHAPTER 11

Pirate

SPENDING MY EXTRA TIME WITH DELIA IS BECOMING ALL I want to do. For the first time since I left the military, it feels like I can just breathe.

"Pirate, you ready to roll?" Shyne asks, pulling on his hoodie.

"Yeah, let me get my phone and we can get on the road." We had just finished putting in one of the sports betting boards and already we've seen an uptick in profit by five percent. It doesn't sound like a lot, but when we're talking about millions of dollars changing hands, five percent is enough to celebrate.

After I grab my phone, Shyne and I head out to make the evening pick up. It's been great finally having him back home. I know he had his reasons for leaving, but the clubhouse just hasn't been the same without him.

We opt to take the truck instead of riding our bikes since I know for sure we're going to have a large amount of cash tonight. There's a medical convention of some sort down in the French Quarter. Even though we may not see all of that crowd, when I had called to check in this morning, our attendance was way up. More tourists mean more people losing money in the casino, which ultimately means more money in our pockets.

"You sure you good to drive?" He asks as we both slide into the cab of the truck.

"Yeah, why wouldn't I be good to drive?" I turn to look at him for a second before I back out of the space and ease onto the dirt road that leads away from the clubhouse.

"I don't know. I mean, it sounded like you were at war last night. Thought maybe you'd need to give your body a rest."

"Ha!" I bark out my laughter. Lia had come over last night and we were up for a while just enjoying each other's bodies, hard. "Why you so concerned about what I was doing last night? Sounds like you need to get yourself a woman."

"How the hell could I not be concerned? It honestly sounded like the two of you were going to go through the wall."

"If I fuck her just a little harder, we might. I'm working up to it." I joke with him.

"Your old ass better stop before you break a fucking hip." Shyne laughs at me and I punch him in his chest.

"How you holding up being back?" I ask him. I know being nomad is different, but I'm hoping that he didn't like it too much. It'd be fucked up if he decides to leave and join Wire full time.

"Shit, it's the same for me. I'm glad to be home, though. It gets annoying dealing with all those fucking prospects. Speaking of prospects. Are you going to see if Noah wants in?"

"Noah? No way, man. He's not about this life." I shake my head.

"What fucking life is that? Because since I've been back, he's been in the clubhouse with Delia more times than not. He gets along with everyone and from what Yang told me, he can hold his own in a fight. He went up against you, didn't he?" Shyne asks.

"Yeah, but what the fuck does that have to do with him joining up to be one of us?"

"Why are you so against it? This seems like it's more than just not a good fit. You hate him that much?" Shyne squints his eyes at me.

"Not at all. It's not that I don't think he'd be a good brother. I just don't want to risk it." I admit.

"What the fuck does that mean?"

"It means he's my insurance policy. Besides myself, no one takes care of Delia like Noah does. When I wasn't around, he was the one that helped her pick up from her worst. If some shit happens to me, I need to know that someone is going to be around to take care of her. I never want her to be alone."

"That's fucking sweet, but do you honestly think a woman like Delia wouldn't be able to take care of herself? She's a strong woman Pirate." Shyne chuckles.

"You act like I don't fucking know that. I know how strong she is."

"Are you sure? It sounds like you think she's a fragile little flower that would break down at the first sign of trouble. With Noah, with you or without the both of you, Delia is going to be just fine. Besides, what kind of ominous jinx shit is this you talking about today. You planning on fucking dying or some shit like that, because if you are I don't want to be in this fucking truck with you." He says the last bit jokingly, but I'm focused on the rest of his message.

I want to make sure I protect Delia at all times, but I can't keep kid gloves on with her. Things get bad for us sometimes and there may be a time when she's going to have to do things she may not want to do. I know she can handle it. Instead of trying to keep her sheltered, it may be time for me to expose her to more of my life. Especially if I'm trying to officially make her my ol' lady again.

"WE STAYING IN TONIGHT?" Delia asks me when she gets to the clubhouse. Noah's one step behind her.

"Hey man, you guys got anything to eat. I had a shoot this morning and haven't eaten anything since." Noah pushes past me and walks to the back where the kitchen is.

"You know I should just get him a prospect patch and call it a day." I'm thinking about what Shyne had said earlier and realized I'd be cool with it. The only reason I'm saying it out loud to Delia is to see how she feels about it.

"Oh God, could you? He's never going to fucking ask, but he's like a goddamn kid in a candy store. I don't know what the appeal is. Running around with a bunch of stinky, sweaty men in leather." Her head tilts to the side slowly and her eyes run over my body.

"Yup, that's the appeal right there," Corrine calls out to Lia as she walks by us and toward the back where Bones' room is.

Lia laughs before she reaches up for me and kisses me swiftly.

"You'd really be okay with him doing this? When I joined up, you had a fit. I figured you'd feel the same way about Noah joining up."

"When you joined, all I could think about was myself. I was selfish. I didn't understand what it meant to have a family. Now I do. He deserves to understand, too. Besides, I think it's gotten to the point he'll disown me if I try to come over here without him." She rolls her eyes and grabs hold of my hand so we can go upstairs.

"Prez, I have the still images you wanted." Clay calls out as he trudges to the bar where Archer is sitting.

There's been rumors people have seen Bull around town, but the amount of times anyone had actually seen him is far less. He's becoming somewhat of a bogeyman or urban legend.

The two of them look through the photos. Jameson and Gator come up to look over his shoulder.

"Archer, you need me?" I ask. I'll stay for the brief if he wants me to, but right now, all I can think about is getting Delia naked.

"Not yet, we'll fill you in later." He says over his shoulder.

I nod, while I tug Delia behind me toward my room.

"You clumsy bastard." Gator snaps at Clay. He'd dropped the folder with the still pictures he pulled from the CCTV cameras around town.

Delia and I turn back to help them pick up the pictures.

"What the fuck?" She stands up, shakes her head and beelines straight for the door.

"Lia? What's wrong?" I have to jog to catch up to her.

"Get the fuck off me!" she screams loud while swinging a haymaker at my head and I step back in shock. It's not a playful hit. She's trying to do damage. What the hell happened in the last twenty seconds? "I don't want nothing to do with this. I told you to leave it the fuck alone!" She screams louder before she turns back toward the door.

"Delia. Wait!" Noah calls out, and he rushes past me to get to her just as she runs out the door.

I don't know what's going on, but I know I don't want her to walk out of here this way.

Noah walks back in a second later with murder locked in his gaze. He comes straight to me with his fists balled up. He's ready to fight. I still don't know what the fuck I did, but I'm not going to let him beat on me. If he wants to scrap, we can do that.

"Noah, I don't know what the fuck is going on here. But if you think we're going to sit back and let you fight one of our brother's you're out of your mind." Archer says calmly from my side.

"This shit got nothing to do with you."

Archer steps directly in front of me. "I don't give a fuck what it has to do with. You're in my fucking house looking like you're a threat to my family. Either you chill the fuck out or you're going to have to take on all of us." When Noah still doesn't move, Archer closes the distance between them. "Back the fuck up. Now!" He barks at him.

Noah flinches slightly and does as he's told. Archer isn't the type to yell, so to hear him do it is alarming.

"You lied to her?" Noah asks.

I shake my head and look around. I feel like I'm in the fucking Twilight Zone. I'm missing something. "About fucking what?" Even I can hear the confusion in my voice. I haven't lied about anything.

Noah squints his eyes at me and walks around the group of us to the pictures that are still scattered about on the floor. He brings one over to me. "How are you connected with this man?" He points to Bull.

"That's none of your fucking business. This is club shit." Yang sneers at him.

"Someone better make it my fucking business or we all going to have to fight. I'm not letting this fly." He says and drops the photo on the floor.

"It's all of us against you." Archer crosses his arms over his chest. "You'd be a dead man."

"If that's what the fuck it's got to be, then so be it." Noah steps back a few paces, gaining some space for himself, getting ready to fight all of us.

Jameson, Gator, and Clay all step forward, ready to take him down.

"Stop." Archer shakes his head and the three of them move back. "He's an enemy. Someone we've been searching for. He used to run a racing club, but we've already taken all of his people down. He's the only one in the wind."

Noah drops his hands and I watch as all the fight drains from his body. "He's not in the fucking wind and you didn't take all his people down."

"How the hell would you know that?" Jameson asks.

Noah stands up and looks me straight in the face, "Because that's the motherfucker that raped Delia."

CHAPTER 12

Pirate

IT FEELS LIKE AN ATOMIC BOMB HAD JUST GONE OFF IN MY mind. I can hear the words coming out of Noah's mouth and the rest of my brothers asking questions, but I can't move. I can't say anything and worst of all, I can't get the sound of him saying Bull was who'd forced himself on my woman from ringing in my ears.

"Pirate, you need to go check on Delia." Archer says right in front of me. When I don't move, he grabs hold of my kutte and shakes me hard enough to rattle my brain.

It's enough to break me out of the fog. "Pirate, I need you to hold it together, man."

"Hold it together? You want me to fucking hold it together? Did you hear what he just said? That bastard Bull is still fucking attacking us and you want me to hold it together? No, fuck that. I want blood brother. I want to drag his dickless body through the fucking streets."

"I hear you, and when we find him, I'll let you fucking do that, but right now we have to find him. We have to make sure we're right about what we're dealing with. Noah here seems to think that there are more Drift Demons rolling around than we accounted for."

"I don't think they're calling themselves that anymore or they've joined with another group." Noah speaks up.

"What other group?" Bones asks.

The second Archer realizes Noah had information on Bull, he calls everyone out of their rooms. They need to know what's going on in a situation like this.

"I'd seen them around before, but I thought they had all moved out. They call themselves the Purged or some shit like that. I don't know if they report to Bull himself, but they work for him."

"No, this is bullshit. We took care of all those mother-fuckers. Rooster's fucking dead. There's no more Purged!" Jameson snaps out.

"Are you sure?" Yang asks Noah, clearly shocked before he turns to Archer, "Shit, he wouldn't even know."

"I know what I heard. They said some shit about the Purged being gods, about how they're immortal. When I heard the dude say it, I figured he was high out of his fucking mind, but who the hell am I to judge." Noah shrugs.

Finally, my mind kicks into gear and I realize what I'm supposed to be doing. I turn on my heel and walk away from the group of them.

"Pirate, where are you going? We need to hear what he has to say." Gator says from behind me.

"I need to get my woman." It's the only explanation that I'm going to give and it's all they need.

"She's just outside. She promised she wouldn't leave without me." Noah shouts out to me. My insurance policy—I'm happy Delia has him and that he's going to be there with her while I ransack the entire fucking town to find this bastard.

I open the door and see her sitting crossed legged in one of the lounge chairs we have on the front patio.

"Sweetheart?" I call out for her and she turns her head to me.

"I told you not to go looking for him. I don't want to deal with this right now, Jimmy. Why would you do that to me?" She looks away and I walk over to where she is, pick her up, and sit down in her place. I place her on my lap and just hold her for a second.

I don't want her to feel how angry I am and think it's because of her. I still feel the same way I did about her this morning. After a few seconds, I speak, "I didn't go looking for him, Delia. I promise you that. We've had problems with Bull for months. Long before you told me what happened. We thought we'd pushed him out of town, but I guess we were wrong. Bull is one of the people that helped kidnap Tink. He kidnapped and tortured Yang and his woman. Not to mention all the shit he helped Rooster do."

"Rooster?" She questions.

"Yeah, he was the president of another motorcycle club until he went fucking crazy and started a war with all the Wings of Diablo and our allies. Rooster's dead though, that shit I know for sure." I squeeze her thigh lightly.

"Well, the rest of them aren't dead. Someone must have gotten their information wrong." She puts her head down and starts scratching at her wrist hard enough to leave raised marks.

I grab hold of her hands to stop her. "What're you thinking?"

"I'm thinking that you're not going to let this go. I'm thinking this is going to be our fucking crossroads and I'm going to lose you in the process. This is the line. Right here is where my Jimmy ends and Pirate shows up. I don't know if I can be like Daria, Corrine, and the other wives here. Always ready for something bad to happen." She sighs and looks up at me. "When we got divorced, my entire world was nothing but what I had thought was anger and pain. I found out through therapy and talking with other people that it's not just anger, but fear. I'm scared, Jimmy. In the past I used booze and drugs to numb that fear, but I don't have that option any longer. I don't want to be scared, Jimmy."

I hear what she's saying, but I refuse to accept that she wants out of my life. I won't let her go again.

"Delia, I'm so sorry I didn't stay strong for you before. I should've tried to stick it out." When we filed for divorce, I'd thought I was doing the right thing. Yet the more we talk about it, the more I realize just how wrong I was. I feel so guilty. So much shit could have been avoided if I'd just not given up.

"No, Jimmy. You have nothing to be sorry for. You've always been here for me, even when I did my absolute best to push you away. I had to get me together." She moves closer to me and drops her head on my chest. I wrap my arms around her waist. The need to never let her go is so strong, but I can feel her and what we have slipping through my fingers all over again.

"Move in with me." I ask her again. I know what she said before about not wanting to move too fast, but things have changed now. I can protect her here.

"Jimmy, for fuck's sake, we just talked about this." She tries to pull away.

"No, just hear me out. This compound's protected. You won't have to be scared here. If you want to stay in a different room, we can work that out, too. Just be here with me." I don't want to beg her, but I'll do it if it means she'll stay.

"Jimmy, have you forgotten that I've been here when shit has hit the fan in the past? Maybe the guys don't know ... It's nothing but scared people here while y'all are out trying to get rid of the threat. No, that's my answer and it's final." She says and gets up off my lap.

"I can't not go after him, Delia. I want you safe and for you not to be scared, but we can't have Bull running around. That's not safe for anyone. If my club rolls, so do I." I reply.

Delia's eyes snap shut, and she nods her head, "I understand, but I don't want anything to do with it." When she opens those gorgeous blue eyes again, I can see the disappointment.

"You giving up on me, Delia?" I ask, wanting to know now if this is truly going to break us. I had never wanted to have to choose between her and the club, but right now that's what it feels like is happening.

"Never, Jimmy. I just need a little time." She smiles at me before she walks back into the club, leaving me sitting on the lounge chair trying to figure out if I'm willing to lose my second chance with Delia or my family instead.

CHAPTER 13

Delia

Noah and I drive back home in silence.

Usually, he's the one trying to break me out of my funk, but he seems to be in a pissy mood himself.

We get back into the house and instead of sitting with me, he just goes to his room, giving me the silent treatment. My mind is all over the place right now and the last thing I need is for him to be adding to my stress.

He was there with me in the clubhouse. He knows what just happened, so I don't understand why he's acting like this now. I sit on the couch and just stare at the walls for what feels like forever, trying to give him his space before my emotions get the best of me. Instead, I explode.

I jump off the couch and storm into Noah's room. "What the fuck is your problem? Why do you have to be so much of a fucking asshole right now? I'd think this would be the best time for you to be a friend, but instead you're treating me like a damn pariah."

His eyes flash with rage and he stands up from the bed. "No one's treating you like anything, Delia. We're all doing exactly what you want. Always just what the fuck you want." He yells right back at me.

I'm taken aback by his outburst. Me and Noah rarely fight and when we do, it's usually over something stupid like who ate the last yogurt. What he's saying right now is heavy.

"What the fuck is that supposed to mean, Noah? If you got something to say, just say it. I'm not with this candy coated shit." I step further into his face, but he doesn't back down.

"Delia, you know my deal. You know that all my life I've forced myself into a fucking box trying to find people who accept me and want to be part of my life. I have no family, none that want me at least. I have a sister who'd watch me burn to death before she lifted a finger to help me. When we met, you said you were the same. It's a fucking lie."

"What are you talking about? I didn't lie about anything." I lean back and stare at him in disbelief.

"You did." He screams before he clamps his lips together and breathes in deeply through his nose, "You did Delia." He says calmer, "I understand a relationship not working and you needing to better yourself, but Pirate is bending over backwards to prove you're still part of the family. He's doing that now.

The women there accept you for who you are even when you're a bitch to them. All of them want to protect you. They're standing there with open arms waiting for you to come home, but you're so set on doing everything on your own. I wish I had someone to lean on and it fucking kills me to see you have dozens of people in your corner ready to drop everything and help, only for you to choose not to accept it." He releases a sigh and shoves his hands into his pockets.

I open my mouth a few times to give a rebuttal, but everything I think of further proves his point. Am I really just being stubborn by not letting the club take care of me? Pirate is always going out of his way to make me feel like I belong when he doesn't have to.

My shoulders slump down and I cock my head to the side. "I have you to lean on. Right?" I put my arms out and Noah instantly wraps me up in a hug.

"Forever. I'm tired, let's take a nap." He kisses my forehead and we lie down on his bed together. I snuggle against him and wish it's with Jimmy instead.

A LOUD BANG jerks me out of my sleep and I take a second before I realize it's not another nightmare.

Another loud bang comes from the front door, and I hear it swing open. Heavy footsteps come trudging in our direction. Someone's here.

"Shit!" Noah jerks up in the bed and pushes me down onto the floor before he reaches for the knife he keeps stashed on the side of the nightstand. The fire escape is in the living room, meaning there's no way for us to get out of the apartment without going through whoever just broke into our house.

I don't have a weapon, but I'm not just going to sit here and let them hurt Noah, not if I can help it. I lean over and pick up a stick he has propped up in the corner. I don't know what it's used for, but it's sturdy and doesn't seem like it'd break easy. I raise the weapon over my shoulder, getting ready to swing until I watch three men walk into the bedroom. Two of them stand to the side and Bull steps to the front.

"You know, I thought shoving my dick in that tight cunt of yours would be enough to get a rise out of those WOD bastards. Seems like I'm going to have to try a little harder to get their attention. I think I'm going to need your help, my little firecracker." Bull smiles wide and snaps his fingers in my direction. The two men he came in with make their way towards me, but Noah is quick to stand in front of me.

"She's not helping you with shit. I don't give a fuck what kind of problems you have with the Wings of

Diablo, but that shit has nothing to do with her." Noah grunts out.

"You think you're going to stop me? I'm taking her out of this apartment one way or another." He shrugs his shoulders and looks down at his nails picking dirt from the nail bed.

"Over my dead fucking body." Noah spits out.

Bull raises his head and smiles, "I was hoping you'd say that." Quicker than I can react to, Bull pulls a gun from the side of his pants, aims it at Noah and pulls the trigger.

My best friend stumbles backwards twice before he falls down to the ground in a heap.

"No! You fucking bastard! Noah! Oh God!" I fall down and try to press down on the wound in his chest but the blood seeps through my fingers. He's already gone. "Wake up, Noah. Don't you fucking leave me!" I yell down at his body. I hear people walking up behind me, reminding me that I'm still in danger. The sharp knife is still in Noah's limp hand, so I pick it up.

Just as one man reaches down to grab hold of me, I swing the knife around and drive it into his thigh with all my might. He screams out in agony when I yank the knife out.

"You stupid cunt!" The man I just stabbed punches me hard in the face and I stumble slightly. He grabs hold of my hair and I hear Bull calling out in the background.

"Don't fucking kill her. We need her alive."

I wonder for a second who the fuck is we, but that's all the time I can spare. The man I stabbed is trying to pull the knife from my hand. I ram my knee into his balls and the second he lets go of my hair, I swing the hand with the knife straight into the side of his neck.

I stare in shock as the man's eyes go wide and blood gurgles in his mouth. A small trail of it leaks from the wound and he falls to his side, clawing at his throat as if he'd be able to save himself.

My mind goes blank as this image sears itself into my brain. I'd never killed anyone before, hell I'd never even seen anyone killed.

Something heavy and hard hits the back of my head. My vision fades for a second before I feel the world spin and I fall to the ground.

"Why'd you have to go and do that? Now I have to make sure this hurts a lot more than we wanted it to." He leans down and presses the gun to my head. I focus on his face until the darkness closes in on my vision.

I'm at the very edge of consciousness. That space right before you wake up from a deep sleep. I feel my body move and air pass over my face. All I can think about is knowing that my best friend had lost his life, because I was too stubborn to accept the help Jimmy begged me to take.

Jimmy would come looking for me, I'm sure of it. The only problem is he's already told me they don't know where Bull is holding up. They'd look for me, but they're not going to find me. All of Jimmy's resources are going to be for nothing.

I wished I'd listened. If I had, right now I'd be snuggled up close to Jimmy with his powerful arms around me and Noah would finally get to know what it feels like to be in a family. Instead, I'm in the arms of the man that raped me, going who knows where.

At least I got to be with Jimmy during my last days. I just hope the memory of those happy times is enough to get me through whatever horrible trauma awaits me.

CHAPTER 14

PIRATE

"I thought the ones with Rooster were the last of the Purged. Why the fuck are we hearing about them again?" Archer drags his hand through his hair.

"You think it's a copycat group or something? Maybe someone's trying to make it seem like they were once part of the Purged to disguise who they're really working for?" Yang asks.

"I don't give a damn if they're copycats or not. If they're running around with Bull, then it makes them just as fucking dangerous. I want every piece of information we can get about who might be part of this shit. Gator and Clay, I don't care if you have to manually search through every fucking piece of footage we get. I want to see who Bull is working with. If he's dumb enough to get caught on tape once, it just means he's dumb enough to get caught on tape with his crew." He turns to Jameson, who's standing by waiting for a directive. "You get on the fucking phone and talk to Nitro. Find out what he knows about another group of the Purged."

Jameson nods his head and walks off to do what he's ordered to do.

"Prez …" I hear Bones call out, but Archer doesn't respond.

"Pirate, I know shit is hard with Delia right now, but I need you to get her to …"

"Archer!" Bones yells out, getting everyone's attention. "Incoming!" He says, but instead of going out the door, he runs toward us, "Get down!"

We all drop and a loud skidding sounds outside followed by a crash to the side of the building. The sound of the women screaming draws my attention. "Clay get over there and check on them." Archer orders.

"Fuck! What the hell was that?" Lex calls out.

"It was a truck." Bones grits out as he pushes himself off the ground.

Another round of pounding echoes through the compound, but this is from the front door. "Pirate!"

A cold sweat springs up on the back of my neck. I jump off the ground and run to the door. It's Noah.

"Shit, wait! You don't know what's going on." Archer calls from behind me.

I don't care what's going on. There's no reason for Noah to be here unless something had happened. Did something happen to Delia? I swing the door open and Noah looks like he's risen from the dead. He's pale and sweating, and his clothes are full of blood.

"What the fuck?" Lex sees him over my shoulder.

"Pirate, he took her. Bull fucking took Delia." He slurs out. Lex and Gator rush up to support him.

My heart has yet to resume beating in my chest. This can't be fucking happening. I run and get in front of him, stopping the three of them from walking any further inside.

"What the fuck do you mean he took her! You were supposed to protect her! How could you fucking let him take her?" I grab hold of his collar.

"I tried! You fucking idiot. I tried everything I could. Did you?" He grunts out. He's barely breathing, but he still has enough fire inside to chew me out. "You knew there was a threat and you let her go, anyway. I don't care if she would've been mad or if you two would've fought, you should've cuffed her to the fucking chair if you had to. Now get the fuck out of my face and go find my best friend, so I can die in peace." He grumbles.

"None of that shit, kid. You're not dying today." Lex replies and walks around me.

"Daria, bring Lex the first aid kit." Archer orders.

I stand there with Noah's blood painting my fingers, kicking myself for not doing exactly what he just said. I should've been stronger. If I wasn't so concerned with winning her back, I would have been able to keep her safe. I'd failed her again.

"Stop it. Right now." Celine walks up to me.

"You don't understand. I knew some shit like this was going to fucking happen." I dig my hands in my hair and pull hard.

"She knew what she needed to do for herself. You can't fucking control that bastard Bull or what he'll do to get to us. You need to be strong for her now. She needs you and not someone just running off without a plan." Celine grabs hold of my arm and gives it a slight squeeze before she walks off, probably to help Lex

"Pirate, brother. Come on. Let's find your woman." Yang calls me over.

I turn my head to the door and then turn back to look at him. I feel so conflicted. Most of me just wants to go out with a fucking torch and set the town on fire until I get Lia back in my arms. Yet the logical part of me knows that running out to kill anything that moves would do nothing but ensure that we never find her. As much as I don't want to even think about what he's doing to her right now, I need to depend on my brothers to help me through this.

Hours have passed and even though we're all working to figure this out, we've got no new leads. Archer had to call in an outside doctor who helps us out from time to time. The doc took Noah to the hospital using fake information. He'd tried to patch up Noah here, but he needed surgery to dislodge the bullet from his chest. The operation went well, but he's still unconscious.

Bones, Shyne, and I all went to Noah's apartment. We only find a dead man laying on the bed. Someone had gone to town on him with a knife. I'm assuming that was my girl. After we get a sight of the destruction in the house, I'm practically useless. All I can think about is him touching her, hurting her, and finally her calling for me to help her. I don't think I've ever felt this help-less in my life. When we get back to the clubhouse, I just sit waiting for someone to tell me what to do.

"Luke!" Daria comes running out of the room, but stops short.

"What is it? Speak." He's short with her, but I'm sure she'd never hold it against him, not with everything that's going on right now.

"We got a message."

Everyone's eyes snap up to hers.

"What? From who?" I demand.

"When did it come in?" Yang asks.

"Why didn't any of us get it?" Gator asks, walking up to the side of her.

Within two seconds, all of us converge on Daria, who now looks like she wants to melt into the wall.

"If you motherfuckers don't get the fuck away from my woman, I'm going to rip your fucking spines out through your asses." Archer barks from behind all of us, "How the fuck is she supposed to talk with all you dumbasses jumping down her throat."

"Sorry Darlin'." Jameson takes a step back.

Archer pushes through all of us so he can get to Daria. "Ma chérie, what's going on?"

"There was a notification from our social media. Ever since all that happened with Monica, any time one of us goes missing, I check, just in case." Daria rings her hands. "There's a video. I only saw a second of it." Her eyes jump to mine, "It looks bad," her voice is soft.

My heart drops to my feet. The last time we had got a message via social media, it was of Jameson's ex-wife being murdered. Is that what awaits me now? My body feels like it's about to buckle when I feel an arm wrap around my midsection.

Bones is holding me up, "We don't know what it is, man. Let's check it out." He says and I get my legs back under me. Maybe Bull has some sort of demand.

"Let's get into church." Archer says and we all walk to the back room. I sit in my chair and wait for them to get the computer open and Daria to navigate to the message.

She hits play and leaves, not wanting to see. From the still image on the screen, I don't blame her.

The video starts and the first thing I see is Delia in a chair with some sort of wire wrapped around her body. The sound comes on and I can hear her breathing hard. She has a gag in her mouth, but I see tears in her blue eyes. She's scared.

"What the fuck is that? What the fuck! Fuck! Fuck!" I drop my head down hard onto the table and Archer puts his hand on my shoulder, giving what little support he can.

The buzzing sound of rolling electricity comes through the speaker and then I hear my woman scream in agony. I roar out right along with her.

I can't fucking take this. I need to get to Delia right now. I'm back to my original plan of burning the whole fucking town down.

"The problem with people like you is you think you've won just because you've cut off the head of the snake. What you all fail to realize is that when one of us falls ten more pop up to take the spot."

"What the shit!" Jameson jumps up from his chair and I raise my head to look at the screen again. I watch as René *walks* across the screen.

René, who we'd left buried under a collapsed building and had no fucking legs.

"In case you're wondering what you can do to get this little firecracker back, I'll save you the trouble. Nothing. You see, there's nothing you have that I want to barter for. Nothing you can do to make me change my mind. You took my son, my fight circuit, and my legs. You've taken everything from me. I'll be doing the same to you. I don't care if I have to recruit every merc, slighted member, and shady connection that I have, I will not stop until you all know how I feel."

He walks off and Bull comes back on screen. He leans down, so he's level with whatever is recording. "Hey Pirate, I think I need another taste of this little lady. You don't mind, do you?"

He taunts me through the lens as he pulls the wires off Delia and throws her down to the ground. The sound of her muffled screams is the last thing I hear as the footage goes black.

René is back, and he's got my ol' lady. He wants me to know what it feels like to lose everything and he succeeded.

CHAPTER 15

Pirate

THE SECOND THE VIDEO IS OVER, ARCHER ORDERS US TO put muscle behind our words. He'd sent us into town to rough up anyone we thought might know anything about where Bull or Rene may be.

We weren't getting anywhere, but at least it was giving me something to do.

Shyne and I go to a car repair shop on the west side of town. Emery is a talented mechanic, but he also has quite the fucking gambling addiction. He uses his shop as a chop shop to make extra cash on the side to feed his need to gamble.

So far, he really hasn't bothered us much, but we know he runs around with a bunch of unsavory people. If there's anyone that might know where a bunch of car junkies are holed up, it's him.

"I don't think you want to get on the wrong side of our club right now Emery! Tell me what the fuck you know!" I roar out and he just shakes his head again.

"Man, I swear I already told you everything I know. About six months ago, I did some work on their cars, but they never came back. Hell those assholes never even came back to pay the balance on their bill. I don't know anything else. Archer and the rest of you boys have been good to me. I'd tell you more if I knew more."

Shyne puts a hand on my shoulder. I've been destroying his place and threatening him for over half an hour. He may really be telling the truth.

"We're not getting anything here. Let's go back to the clubhouse." Shyne tries to pull me away, but I just rip my arm away from him.

"What the hell for? She's not fucking there." I fist my hands against my temples and try to stop the unbearable pounding in my head. All I can hear is the sound of her screaming in pain.

This feels like karma is playing a cruel joke on me. I finally get my woman back into my life and then a bastard we had thought was under control comes back and takes her away from me.

My phone rings in my pocket and I'm slow to reach for it. Every time it goes off it makes me feel like someone is calling to tell me more bad news, like they found Delia's body and they need me to come pick it up. I look down at the number on the screen to see that it's Lex.

"Yeah, brother."

"Pirate, Noah's up. He's asking about Delia. Do you want us to go talk to him or do you? Maybe he has more information? See if he noticed anything about what happened in the apartment?" I hear the rev of his bike on the line. He's on the move, probably following up another lead for me.

"Yeah, I'll go. He should hear it from me, anyway." I hang up the phone and just walk out of the repair shop like we hadn't just traumatized this man to within an inch of his life.

"We through here?" Shyne asks.

I nod without looking back. I hear him saying something to Emery, probably trying to smooth shit over. Only I don't have time to deal with that. I've got to go tell Noah we still haven't found Delia and from the way it looks, we're not going to find her soon.

NOAH IS in a private room in the hospital. He's listed under a false name, Mr. Nick McCary. It doesn't fit him at all.

I knock on the door lightly when I see him sleeping. His eyes pop open right away.

"Hey man, where you been?" Noah croaks out and tries to sit up. This is the first time since I've seen him where he doesn't look like they carved him out of a fucking magazine—no designer clothes, hippie hats, or perfectly coiffed hair. He looks fucked up, if I'm honest.

"Sorry, we've been out trying to find Lia." I say.

Shyne's here with me as well, but he doesn't come further into the room. "Pirate, I'm going to head downstairs. Work on getting more information. I'll be there when you're ready to go."

I nod, silently thanking him for the privacy.

"Hey Noah, good shit not dying." Shyne smirks before he leaves the room.

"Doesn't he know that the pretty people never die? It would throw off the balance of the cosmos." He chuckles and I have to stop myself from punching him right in the face for saying some conceited shit like that.

"Yeah …" I look down, not able to join him in the laughter. He may know that Delia is missing, but he knows nothing else. He wasn't there when we got the video message.

"Shit is still bad, isn't it?" He asks, his voice somber again.

"Yeah man. Shit is still fucked up." I hear my voice crack, but I clear my throat.

"What do we know? Has anyone heard anything from her or Bull?" Noah forces himself to sit up in the bed now. Completely focused on the information that I might know.

"We know that it's definitely one of our enemies that has her. He's not someone we can negotiate with. He doesn't want anything besides to make our lives hell. I shouldn't have …" I clamp my mouth shut and shake my head in disgust.

"You shouldn't have what?" Noah asks.

"I shouldn't have been trying to get with Delia while we still had all this shit going on. Maybe Bull and René would have overlooked her. Maybe she would be home fucking safe right now. I don't fucking know. All I know is that the longer they have her, the more I feel like I'm dying inside and it's my fault this is happening." I let out a deep sigh and see him staring at me like I have a booger hanging out of my nose.

"You not good with timelines, huh?"

"Excuse me?" I squint my eyes at him.

"Timelines, because you're over here talking about how you shouldn't have been trying to get with her. Pirate, Bull raped her before you were ever back in the picture and when he came in to get her from the apartment, he said that he thought it would catch your attention sooner. You and her getting back together had nothing to do with what they were going to do with her. They were going to do it either way. The only difference is now you know what's going on, whereas if you and her didn't get back together and she stayed trying to only do shit on her own, you'd never have known until it was too late. Stop trying to be the fucking martyr and get your head out of your ass." He coughs once before he leans back slightly against the pillow.

"It may already be too late." I admit to him.

He leans back up again. "What does that mean? Are you telling me she's ..." He leaves off the last of his statement, too scared to say the word dead.

"No, well, at least we don't think she's dead. But they're hurting her. We got a message after you went into surgery. It's from Bull and René."

"A message? What kind of message? Let me see it." He raises his voice, agitated that I've kept this news from him.

"You don't want to see it, man. I didn't even want to fucking see it. It's not good. Just them beating her and telling us we're never going to see her again no matter what we do. There's no way for us to stop them and that he's going to make sure we suffer the same way we made him suffer. The man is out of his mind. We should have taken care of him when we had the chance, but we didn't." I do my best to tell him as much detail as I can so I don't have to replay that video. As it stands, I'm going to have recurring nightmares about what I saw.

He glares at me for a second. "Let me see the fucking video."

"Noah."

"I said let me fucking see it!" He shouts at me and the alarms for his heart monitor go off.

"Chill, all right." I put my hands up trying to calm him down and in that second, the nurse comes rushing to the door.

"Mr. McCary, are you okay? Your monitor went off. Do you need more pain medication?" She asks the usual questions, all while shooting me accusatory looks.

"No, I'm fine." He gives her a small half smile, and the woman blushes hard. He's really a ladies' man, even when he has a fucking bullet hole in his chest.

I wait for the nurse to leave before I pull out my phone. I'm not looking forward to seeing this shit again. Fuck, I don't even want to hear it, but I don't really have much of a choice.

I find the mp4 file that Daria had forwarded to all of our phones and play it for Noah. Tears stream down his face when he sees what they're doing to her, but then he does something that I wasn't expecting. He rewinds it and watches it again. By the third time that he plays it, I want to throw his ass out of the window.

"What the fuck are you doing? Why the hell are you watching it over and over? What he says isn't going to magically fucking change. Give me my fucking phone. I don't want to hear her screaming anymore."

"I know where this is." Noah completely ignores what I'm saying and rewinds the video again.

"What?"

He watches the video one more time and I see him mouthing shit to himself and his eyes jerking from side to side like he's reading something that isn't there.

"Bro, you all right? You need me to call the nurse?" Maybe he's having a seizure or some shit. This probably pushed him too far over the edge. I wouldn't blame him. Not only did he almost fucking die, but now he has to watch his best friend being tortured and possibly raped again.

"This is on the second sublevel under the Empress Ladies strip club on Delta Lane and New Cannon Street." He says with absolute certainty.

"What the fuck? How the hell do you figure that shit? That place has been closed and condemned for years. You can't even get in there."

"You can. There is a sewage entrance about two blocks away that'll take you right there. I'm sure the guards will be at the door, but you have guns for people like that."

"How the hell do you know that?" My chest aches from the heaving breaths I'm taking in. The entire background of the video is just one gray concrete wall and two water pipes. There are no identifying features, no banners, and no windows, nothing that could point to the fact that this is indeed where he is saying she is.

"I have a photographic memory. It's a burden and why I turned to drinking and drugs, but it comes in handy sometimes. It's why those guys were trying to jump me a while back." He explains.

"What do you mean? How does you having a photo-graphic memory help them?" I'd heard of people with photographic memories, but I'd assumed that just meant they recalled information better. I'm not seeing how that would cause a group of men to want to beat him down.

"Photographic memory means I pretty much remember everything I see, like which cards have already come out of the deck in a blackjack game.

Sorry Pirate, but before I met you, me and those guys were ripping you the fuck off. I count cards. It's how I get the money I need to keep my modeling career afloat. You think I got gigs and agents banging down my door. I go to casinos, win enough money to get me through for a while. I had a standing agreement with them, but after I met you and the rest of the club, I felt like shit and didn't want to do it anymore. Hence me getting my ass kicked."

I should ring his fucking neck. Technically, he's been stealing from the club. I don't have time to be mad about it now. "Fucking slimy piece of shit. But what does that have to do with you knowing where this is." I turn my phone around so he can see the screen.

"I've been there before, the numbers on the stand-pipes. I memorized them. That is where they are."

I stare at him for a few seconds, trying desperately not to get my hopes up. This can't be this fucking easy. "Don't fuck around, are you sure?"

"Yeah man, now go fucking get her. Pirate. Please. Just get her." He begs me and I don't bother to reply. Instead, I rush out the door of the hospital with my phone already in my hand, calling Archer to let him know that we have the first genuine lead that we've had all night. I just hope we make it there in time.

CHAPTER 16

Pirate

Everyone rides out fully armed and ready to take down whatever we find.

"He's really been scamming us?" Yang asks me through the in-helmet headset. The drive to the old strip club is about forty minutes and even with us going at top speed, we take longer than I like to get there.

"Apparently, he was able to set up a nice little agreement using his skill. We can deal with that later. Right now I just want to focus on getting to this fucking place."

"Pirate, are you sure that we can trust this man? He did just admit that he was stealing from us. Do you think he had anything to do with Bull being able to take Delia?" Archer is the one to ask.

"No way. Not the way he loves that girl."

"Yeah, I can't see him doing that shit." Bones says. "He's a good guy."

It's not lost on me that pretty much everyone in the club seems to like Noah, even though he can be a fucking prick sometimes. I hope we get through this. I really think he'd make a great prospect. Plus, I get to fuck with him while he takes that long run.

"We should park up here. Didn't he say there was a sewer entrance two blocks away? We should be close and we don't want any of Bull's people to see us rolling up on them." Jameson says, drawing me out of my daydream.

"Agreed. Let's park up. I want everyone fully fucking protected. Bring your main weapon and a sidearm." Archer spits out his orders and everyone falls in behind him until we park our rides.

"Keep this shit quiet if we can. I don't know if there are any other civilians down there, but we don't take any chances. Put these bastards down and we'll sort out any fucking problems later." Archer gestures for Gator to open the manhole cover.

I can see the old strip club from where we are. It's dark, and they'd boarded the windows up. There is an enormous sculpture of a woman with her legs kicked straight up on the roof of the building. The neon that used to make her glow doesn't work anymore, but it's a prime spot for a sniper. If I were Bull, I would've made sure there's someone up there to keep watch. I guess we're lucky that he's not as smart as we are.

We get down into the sewer and slowly make our way through the rank smelling tunnel. The tunnel only goes in one direction, so we can't get lost. There are ladders and entry points every couple of hundred feet. The first one goes up very high and leads back up into the street level. The second one has a shorter ladder and when we open it to look through, we see the inside of a building.

Noah was right about the sewer leading into the club. It must have been built into the basement for any flood waters.

"Keep fucking quiet and make sure that your locator beacons are on." Archer hisses at us.

I nod and force myself to take slow, steady breaths. I don't hear anything. What if we're too late? What if she's up there right now, dead in the corner? I don't know how the fuck I'd survive some shit like that.

"Stay on my hip, brother. We're right here with you." Shyne says as he goes up the ladder ahead of me. He had just spent the last few months trying to find his cousin. Even though I know his feelings are not the same for Tink, I believe he knows at least part of what I'm going through right now.

We make our way up and out of the sewer into a dark room.

"Something's off." Archer speaks as we all continue to move through the room.

"What?" Yang asks.

"No fucking resistance. There should have at least been someone in this room. Shit is fishy."

"Fuck, you think it's a trap?" Jameson asks.

"Be ready for anything." Our president snaps out.

The room we're in is filled with boxes and old furniture. Nothing seems to have been moved since this place closed down. They coated the walls in an ugly off red paint that's chipped showing the gray concrete wall underneath it. This isn't the room Delia was in. There must be another spot they are keeping her.

"There's a door here." Gator calls out.

We all take up a defensive perimeter, keeping each other in our line of sight. Following him through the door into a long, dark hallway spacious enough for us to walk through and leads to another door. The carpet smells like old water that's been sitting for years. I can taste it in the back of my throat. Bones is the one to open this door. He stops for a second and looks back at us.

"She's not here." He says before he walks into the room.

This is the place. I see an overturned chair. I see the standstill pipes Noah could identify. The wires and car batteries he'd used to torture Delia are still here. This is the place, but my woman isn't fucking here.

"No, what the fuck! Where are they?" I pace back and forth, trying to find some sort of clue which way they went.

Did they just leave? Have they killed her and are just finding somewhere to dump the body? What the fuck did we miss?

"Did we get any other message?" I turn to Archer, but he just shakes his head.

René said that we wouldn't. He said there was nothing we could do to change his mind. He's not going to give us hints about where she is. He's just going to fucking kill her.

"Fuck!" I roar out and punch my hand into the wall. I let my head fall forward and my eyes focus on the ground. Another fucking dead end. Everyone keeps fucking saying this isn't my fault, but I can't stop thinking about how much they're all wrong. It's me that introduced her to this life that she didn't want to be in and me that couldn't keep her safe when my enemies came for her.

"What the hell is that?" Yang says, holding up his flashlight.

I turn around quickly to see him looking at the ground. My sight focuses in on the floor, but I only see a fucked up paint job.

"It's the fucking floor Yang." I say.

"No, it says something. I need to get higher. I can't see …" He rushes around the room and starts stacking shit so he can climb on it to get to higher ground. I see nothing but swipes of paint. It looks like something abstract.

The rest of us point our flashlights at the floor to give him more light. "Kansas …" Yang's eyebrows cinch together until he looks back up at the group of us, "What the fuck is Kansas City Shuffle?"

"What? Is that what it says?" I scurry over to where Yang is and push him out of the way so I can make sure. The second I look down from a greater height, I see the words.

Lex groans out and his head drops back. "Fuck! We need to get the hell out of here right now."

It seems like he and I are the only ones who know what the fuck a Kansas City shuffle is. Being the old heads of the club, it makes sense.

"Hold the fuck up. What does it mean?" Archer asks.

"Kansas city shuffle is a con. Basically, the con man gets the mark to believe that they are being involved in a trick or game. The victim sees it and thinks they've figured out how to beat the trick, then while the mark is so focused on beating the trick or con, the con man has actually been pulling a completely different trick without the victim noticing." I do my best to explain.

"It's a fucking bait and switch. This is a damn trap, it's just not for us." Lex says as he walks out the room.

Oh God. What have we done?

"Archer, who's home? Clay's the only one protecting the clubhouse." I tell him, herding him to the door.

His eyes go wide when he realizes what I'm saying. We are all out here looking for Delia. We'd left Clay at the clubhouse to watch over the ladies, but if all the opposition we thought we would find here is there, he's not going to be able to hold them off alone. Not only did we leave our brother to fight a war on his own, but we left the ol' ladies there too.

"Move!" Archer orders as we all run out of the underground location.

I call Clay the second I get out of the sewer, but there's no answer. "Clay's not answering."

"Call the fucking clubhouse phone." Jameson barks out.

I hit the speed dial icon for the clubhouse and it just rings. "No answer."

"Motherfuckers!" Archer bellows as we all get to our bikes and race back home.

Did we just lose half of our family just to get back one member?

ARCHER CALLS Clay and Daria more than a dozen times, trying to get in contact with them while we're on the road. It's the longest fucking ride of my life.

When we get home, the door is open. The first fucking sign that shit had already gone bad.

Archer jumps off his bike, not even bothering to engage the kickstand, and runs into the club. He doesn't wait for any of us to catch up to him and watch his back.

"Everyone fucking be ready, they may still be on site!" Gator says. He's the only one who has his head on straight right now. All the rest of us are crazed as we run in to see if Bull and his Drift Demons have really taken everything away from not only me, but the rest of my club.

"Daria!" Archer yells out and runs to their room.

I look around the compound and see a flurry of bullet holes. I see two bodies, but they don't belong to the Drift Demons. They are wearing Purged kuttes. I guess they're not as taken cared of as we had thought.

Jameson, Yang, Bones, and Lex all go running around trying to find the women and Clay, but there is no sign of anyone. While we were off running to find Delia, those bastards had walked into our fucking house and pulled our family from their beds like it was nothing.

"I'll fucking kill them all! What the fuck is going on!" Archer looks around the clubhouse with his hands tugging at his hair.

"Every damn bone in their body. I'll pull out every fucking bone in their bodies before they hurt her." Bones says more to himself than to any of us.

Jameson is upstairs in his room, throwing his shit around. Yang is doing the same. Now it's not just one of us at a complete loss, it's all of us. How the fuck do we focus on finding René when we can't go a second without thinking about what he's doing to our women. Celine told us the fucked up shit he had planned for her when he took her for Matthew. The man's so deep in the underworld, we didn't even realize just how strong he was getting. We thought that by killing Rooster, he would go back into hiding. Instead, now he's stronger than ever.

Archer grits out a low moan and scrubs his hand down his face. The calm, level-headed man that we depend on is gone. Instead, I only see a fucking killer in front of me. He doesn't say a word to anyone, just goes straight for the front door.

"Where are you going, Prez?" I call out behind him. I'd never take him for someone to abandon his patch.

"Noah did this. He sent us into that fucking trap."

My mind spins at his words. "What? How the fuck did you get that?" The rest of the club is on his tail, everyone jumping on their bikes and Archer bending down to pick his up.

I grab hold of his arm, and he takes my wrist into his hand. In a move I've never seen done, he bends my fingers back and, using only momentum, flips me so I'm on my back on the ground. He pulls his weapon out and shoves it in my face.

"Noah's the only fucking one to point us in that direction. He's the one to get us moving. It was a trap and we wouldn't have fucking gotten caught in it if we didn't follow his fucking directions. I don't know if he's with them or not, but unless he has a good fucking way to get my woman back in my goddamn hands I'm going to blow his fucking head off. Guilty or not. You want to stop me? You can take his place." Archer stares at me, waiting for me to say something.

Only I have nothing I can say to erase the pain and anger inside the man.

He steps over me, and once again rights his bike. I get myself off the ground and rush to mine. I can't do anything here, but hope Noah has a way to figure out where René and our women are. I don't want to believe he's behind us falling into this trap, but if he is, I have a feeling Archer and the rest of the boys are going to have a good time getting some payback.

CHAPTER 17

Pirate

"Get him outside now." Archer growls into the phone as the group of us park behind the hospital that Noah is in. We can't go upstairs and just pull him out of the room so Archer gets his doctor friend to set up a transfer. A transfer from the hospital right into our care.

A few minutes pass and I check my phone constantly in case René decides he wants to leave any more messages. Nothing has come through and no one is calling our phone with any updates. We're at a fucking standstill.

"What the hell is going on?" I hear Noah say through the door. It opens and the doctor walks him out. He's wearing nothing, but the hospital gown and some non-slip socks.

He sees all of us, but doesn't crack a smile, "Pirate? What the fuck is this?"

I open my mouth to talk, but Archer speaks up first, "Shut your fucking mouth Pirate."

I do as I'm told.

"Bones, get our friend. We're going for a walk." Archer says.

Bones hops off his bike with Lex by his side. They grab hold of Noah who struggles but not much. He's still very weak from the bullet wound.

"What the hell is wrong with you assholes?" Noah asks, but doesn't get a reply from anyone. It's the silent treatment right now.

I want to scream at the top of my lungs that we're wasting time. Except Archer's word is law if he wants to skin this man before he asks him a question I can't do anything to stop that no matter how badly I might want to. I still believe that Noah cares way too much about Delia to be in on her kidnapping, but on the other hand I know that he was having money problems. He owes someone something. Maybe he'd thought this was the easiest way to get out of trouble.

We make our way to one of the trailers the hospital uses for community outreach. They are still on hospital ground, but right now there's no one inside of them. It gives us a little bit of privacy all without having to move Noah too far. Bones pushes him inside and the rest of us crowd into a space that's clearly only designed for a few people.

"Did you fucking set us up Noah?" Archer ask, his voice is low and deadly.

"How? Seriously, how the fuck would I set you up?" Noah says, wheezing a few times and leans against the chair Bones dropped him against.

This particular trailer is for dental work so there are a few small tools in here including a small scalpel. It's not much, but I'm sure it'd do some real damage when needed, Archer presses the blade to his face, "You know pretty boy, you've only just gotten to be around us. You don't know the length the Wings of Diablo will go to in order to protect our family. No police, government, or moral compass is going to stop us from finding them. Right now the only connection is you. It was your tip that led us into that trap. So now you're going to tell me where our people are."

"Archer, you're absolutely right. I just got here and I do know the lengths you'd go through, because I'm pretty sure that I'd go to the same lengths if I had a family to do it for. The only family I have is Delia and I did everything physically and mentally possible to help find her. I don't know what fuck you're talking about a trap or what you plan on doing to me, because of it. But if you could hurry the fuck—" Noah doesn't have the chance to finish his sentence. Archer grabs him by the front of the gown and punches him in the face. Noah's body whips backward, but Archer holds on to the thin material to pull Noah back forward so he can punch him in the face again. The second punch has blood spewing out of his nose and mouth.

"You think this is a fucking game? Tell me where the fuck they are."

Noah shakes his head, "Tell you where the fuck who are? For a bunch of people who are supposed to have your shit together you sure don't know what the fuck you're doing? How am I supposed to give you answers to some shit I don't know about." He wheezes hard and leans back against the chair Archer just dropped him in.

"Where the fuck are our women?" My president screams at him.

Noah's eyebrows scrunch together and he looks at me, "What are you talking about women? I thought you were looking for Delia."

"We were, but as we were running down the lead you sent us on, they came back to our clubhouse and took our wives and Clay. They knew we would find that place and waited for us to leave before they made their move." Jameson says.

"Called it a Kansas City Shuffle." Yang says.

"What? You're fucking shitting me. You got played by Joshua? First of all, let's address me being a fucking rat or liar or whatever the fuck you think I am. If you're just going to hit me, we're not going to get anywhere. Also, I know women like ruggedness, but I don't pull that off well. Leave me pretty."

"Oh, I'm going to leave you pretty alright. You going to be really fucking pretty filleted in my workstation. Your skin will look great in a frame on my wall." Bones snarls at him.

"Well fuck, that's probably the worst damn image I've ever had." Noah shivers slightly before he continues, "How the hell would I know? I didn't know Bull was going to shoot me in the chest. I didn't know that he was going to film that shit. How the fuck would he know that I would be able to locate him using only the numbers on the pipe behind him? How would I know that you'd leave yourhouse ungaurded and how would I know that they would come in and take them when I've been in the fucking hospital either almost dead or fucking unconscious until today. You think they did all this shit in the past two hours?" He squints at us for a second before he continues again.

"As far as the fucking Kansas City shuffle, I'd put money on it that Joshua had something to do with it. He's fucking obsessed with everything about that movie *Lucky Number Slevin*. He says that shit all the fucking time. He runs his own schemes and shit in the casinos, but mostly does underground work. The spot where I sent you is his place. That is where he has all of his illegal poker games. It makes sense that your bad guy would have him help get Delia out of there." Noah finishes his speech on a wheeze.

"That doesn't help us to know where they got the phrase from or even where they got help. We still don't know where our people are."

"No, but he may be able to help you find out where they are keeping them. If you're going to kill me, just don't shoot me in the face. Open casket and all." He says and closes his eyes like he is genuinely fine with dying for this cause.

He's right about him not having any type of time to help René and Bull, not when he's been in the hospital all the while. Bull probably thinks he's dead. I don't want to stand in front of my president if he decides to kill him right now, I'm just praying he knows this is wrong.

"You're going to take us to this Joshua and then we'll see if I need to shoot you in the face or not." Archer says before he turns and walks out the trailer.

Luckily, Shyne brought the truck instead of riding his bike to meet up with Noah, because we left the hospital with him. He's bleeding and obviously in pain. Gator and Lex try to make shit more comfortable for him in the truck, but it's not really possible the kid is hurting bad.

We pull up to an apartment building again on Noah's advice.

"He lives here. That black and gray continental is his. He's the only one on his floor, the first floor is a drug den." Noah says between pants.

"Get up, you're taking us to him." Archer grunted out.

This is too much, the man can barely walk. He's already taken a bullet for my woman and now my club is about to push him past his limit simply because they don't know if they can trust him. "Prez, I want to find them as much as you do, but you're going to kill him before we can. He's fucked up enough."

"If you question me again Pirate, I'll take your patch and beat you the fuck out of my club. If I want him spit roasted right now that's what the fuck I'll do." Archer stares me down for a second as we wait for Shyne and Gator to get Noah out of the car.

He screams out in agony as he takes a step out of the car. I watch as Noah uses the car to right himself the best he can. "So are we waiting on the real estate brothers or are we going in?" Noah quips half-heartedly raising one eyebrow. Always with the fucking jokes.

"You a real fucking joker, Noah. I wonder how many jokes you going to have when we are beating your face in." Archer snarls from behind him.

For the first time since I've joined the club, I'm ashamed to call Archer my president. He's gone, not thinking clearly and frankly putting all of us in danger.

"Yeah, I got a few special ones for the occasion. A lot in the knock knock variety." Noah says.

"Noah, shut up!" I bark at him. There's no way that he can be taking this shit seriously or if he is then the man really doesn't give a fuck if he dies or not.

He listens to me and we walk into the semi-lit building. "He's on the second floor." Noah huffs and tries to take a step, but collapses right away.

"Get up!" Archer orders.

"Fuck this." I move around everyone else and pick Noah up. "Come on. Let's go." I take the brunt of his weight so he barely has to put his feet down as we ascend the stairs.

"If he sees you he won't open the door. Let me go first." Noah says, his face is taking on that pale color again and looks like he may pass out at any second.

"Fuck that, he could be tipping whoever is behind the door off. This could be a trap again." Bones offers up this nugget of wisdom.

"Are you fucking serious?" Noah grumbles.

I push Archer behind me and draw my weapon just in case. "We won't move until we know it's just him." I whisper.

"Y'all straight yet?" Noah leans hard against the door frame.

"Go." Archer says from behind me.

Noah knocks on the door, then after a second he does a knock that people use as a password, it has a melody to it.

"Who is it?" A voice calls out.

"It's Noah, the dream boat. I got jumped. Let me in." Noah says, not necessarily lying.

"Jumped? Aww man, I told you about fucking with those married women. You're not going to fucking believe what I did today." The door opens, but the man inside doesn't step out. "Oh fuck man, you don't need to be here you need to go to the hospital."

"Can you get me some water?" Noah asks, but then walks further in the doorway. We can't see inside so there's no way for us to determine if it's a trap or anything like that.

I almost reach out and grab Noah, but I watch his fingers disengage the slam lock on the door. He's giving us a way to get in. The door slams and I hear the man inside talking. I move forward slightly with Archer and Jameson at my back.

"Easy. Stay low." Archer orders and I do what he says. I turn the knob and the door opens easily. I don't push it all the way open just enough to peek inside. Yang hustles to the other side of the door and looks through the small slit the open door gives us.

"It's just them I think. I don't see anyone else." Yang says.

"What you got into? You look keyed the fuck up like you on the good side of an eight ball." I hear Noah say.

"Noah, you should have been around! I had a client come in earlier, I can't tell you who, but he used to be the fucking king of underground fighting. You couldn't even get tickets to see one of the fights he put on. Anyway he shows up looking for a place to run a little command center or some shit off the grid and you know I have all the fucking off the grid locations under lock and key. Speaking of lock and key, did you lock the door?"

"Yeah man, the slam locks on. And slow down you speaking like you got the fucking energizer bunny in your asshole." Noah jokes.

"Oh, right my bad. I'm just excited! Yeah, I bring him down there and he has like a whole fucking crew with him. So of course I'm like fuck yeah, I'm going to get in where it's good. These aren't some low level thugs either. The main guy is one of those racer assholes that has connections all over the place. If he signs off on me I could be running a hustle all over town. It's like money on top of money just waiting for me."

"Shit man. Sounds like you got your work cut out for you. You going to roll with them or what?" Noah asks.

"Fuck yes. I'm not like you Noah. The fucking loner. I don't think you've ever met anyone you like enough to spend more than a day with. I want to have some back up." Joshua says.

"I don't think you picked the right backup." Noah says before a round of coughing wracks his body.

"Fuck yes I did! They're fucking gold! I had to let them use my other spot, but they going to cut me in. They getting ready to take over NOLA."

"You told them about the Kansas City …" Noah groans and I turn to look at Archer basically willing him to order us in. The kid is going to die.

"Damn right! Finally got to use it! That bait and switch will never fail! I don't know why more people aren't … wait a minute, how'd you know? Are you a narc! What the fuck!"

I can hear the man panicking inside. This is about to get much worse than it already is.

"Prez, we need to move." Shyne spits out.

Archer simply turns his head and glares at Shyne. We're not doing shit according to him.

"Oh fuck, just not the face." I hear Noah say.

"He pulled a weapon," Yang says from where he is giving us play by play with what's going on inside.

"Now, go." Archer pats my shoulder and we all rush into the fucking apartment. Half of us go to where Joshua and Noah are sitting while the rest go around the apartment just to double check no one's there.

"Oh shit! What the fuck is this? You need a warrant. I want my lawyer, I'm not telling you shit!" Joshua screeches as he fumbles with the gun and drops it on the ground.

"You've told us all we need to know. You going to tell me one more thing before you die. What other spot did you tell your new crew about?" Archer asks.

"I'm not telling you nothing!" Joshua's pupils are enlarged and he's fidgeting all over the place.

"Not today, I don't have fucking patience for this shit." Bones grabs hold of him and drags him to the kitchen. "Jameson hold him."

"You crazy bastards. Let go of me!" The man yells out.

"Where is the other spot?" Bones asks.

"Fuck you!" Joshua laughs as the words roll off his tongue, but Bones is already making moves. He grabs the man's arm in a vice grip and shoves it in the sink drain.

"Jameson, cover his mouth." Bones orders right before he reaches over and activates the garbage disposal. Blood splatters all over the placc, I hear the machinery grinding and working hard to get through the man's fingers.

"Oh well, he's not going to be pulling any smash and grabs any time soon." Noah says weakly.

Bones pulls the man's mangled fingers out of the garbage disposal, and Jameson let's go of his mouth. Joshua cries and shakes in Jameson's grasp. "Noah, help me! Don't let them do this!" The man calls out.

"Sure, sure, let me give you a hand." Noah replies.

No one says anything, but I hear a distinct grating sound like someone is trying to hold in a laugh. I turn my head to see Lex turning a bright red and then he puts a hand over his mouth trying to hide his laughter again.

"Even in fucking death." Archer shakes his head before he looks over his shoulder at Noah. "Lex,

Shyne, Gator. There's a first aid kit in the back of the truck, get him fixed up enough to get back to the hospital. I'll let the Doc know he's on the way."

I breathe a sigh of relief as the three of them work fast to get Noah where they can help him.

"Wait! I need to know where Delia is." Noah grits out.

"We'll find her." I say, it'a promise if I ever heard one. Noah nods and all but collapses against Lex.

"Where the fuck is the other spot?" Bones doesn't take a break, he grabs Joshua's other hand and shoves it into the garbage disposal.

"It's at the Ridgeco Development site." He yells out.

"Bullshit, that site was defunded. They never finished building up the houses. The fuckingswamp has damn near taken it over."

"It's there. The foundations were built, basements, cellars. I use it all the time. Please let me go. That's all I know." The man cries leaning back against Jameson's chest.

Bones looks over to Archer waiting on the next directive.

"Kill him, and let's move before they get away again."

Bones picks up a knife and places it on Joshua's throat. Archer is out the door before Bones can finish slicing the blade across the man's neck.

Joshua may not have been a horrible person, but he's just one more person standing between us and our family.

CHAPTER 18

Delia

MY BODY HURTS LIKE I'VE BEEN CRUSHED TO DEATH AND then resuscitated. The electricity is a pain that I've never felt before and hope to never feel again. Bull beat me unconscious after he tried to rape me. The first time I wasn't ready for him. This time with adrenaline coursing through my body I fight harder than I've ever fought before. I would have ripped one of his eyeballs out of his head if I had a bit more time.

I cough and a wad of blood comes up. He must have broken something or I'm bleeding inside, because it's hard to breathe and I can barely walk. Not to mention I have been peeing blood all day.

"Come on, Lia. We need to keep you off the cold floor." Daria pulls me further up on her lap and rubs my hair.

"I'm okay. It's fine." I say.

"Oh, I could kill them for hurting you like this." Corrine says as she sits down by my head and wipes some of the blood off my mouth.

Ice sits on the other side of me by my feet ready to cover me if Bull or one of his cronies comes in. Celine is standing by the door with Clay.

"I can't believe we were so fucking dumb! How could we fall for that?" Celine curses herself.

"We had to help, there's nothing dumb about it." Daria says. "We're not going to sit here and beat ourselves down about what we should or shouldn't have done. We're going to keep calm and stay alive."

Her voice is sweet and soft, but holds all the authority in the room. As Archer's woman Daria knows a little bit about being in charge, but I'd first thought for sure she'd fall to pieces when he wasn't around. She's so much stronger than I had ever thought.

"Move the fuck away from the door." Bull yells out and all of us move back. Clay is the only one to stand in front.

From what the girls had told me they were all tricked. A man ran up to the clubhouse and said that his babies and wife were stuck in the small creek. He'd said something about trying to drive his car through the brush and it flipped. Of course the women all ran out to help even though Clay had said it was strange.

Clay's been protecting them since they got here.

The door opens and Bull and another man walk in. "Time to eat."

"Put the food down." Clay orders.

"I'm not doing shit, those whores can come over here and get it themselves one by one. If they're nice to me I might give them some extra bread." The other man says.

"Fuck you." Clay moves to fight.

"No, it's not worth it. We can get it." Celine puts her hand up to stop Clay and he steps back tentatively.

"That's a good bitch." The man raises his hand and lets the sandwich he was holding for Celine drop to the floor. "Pick it up."

"You disgusting pig!" Ice snaps at him from where she's sitting.

"Keep quiet, or I'll make sure to give you special attention. I have more than just this sandwich I can feed you." He licks his thin lips and turns back to look at Celine. "Now be a good girl and fetch your food."

Celine slowly bends down tothe floor and just like a fucking prick the man picks up his foot and kicks her in the stomach. Clay launches himself at the man. They tussle for a brief second until Bull pulls them apart.

"Drop the food, something is going on up top." Bull presses his finger to his ear like he has someone talking directly into his head.

Clay spits blood at the man before he comes over and checks on Celine. She rolls over holding her stomach but has enough energy to crawl over to us.

"What do you think it is?" Ice asks.

"The boys or if not them, someone they sent." Daria says with all the conviction in the world. I know Pirate is out looking for me, but even I doubt that they would be able to find us. Not Daria though. I would say she doesn't even look scared.

"Archer is lucky to have you." I look up at her doll-like face, those wide eyes staring down at me and a smile spreading across her freckle dusted cheeks.

"Pirate is lucky to have you again. We all are, you two complement each other in ways I never thought possible. I'm happy to have you home." She rubs my hair and I feel a cold chill roll through my body. Something is really messed up inside me, I can feel it.

"Home? Is your home really my home? I've never been anything but the angry ex. Why would that be my home?" My voice is strained when it comes out. I really don't want to cry right now. I know it'll hurt if I do.

"Delia, of course our home is your home. You're family. Just because you two went through a hard time doesn't mean that we forget about you. You needed space, you needed to get through things on your own, and I know everyone supports you in that journey. Whenever you're ready to step through those club-house doors and lay down your head you are forever welcome. You're always going to have family with us." Daria pushes some hair out of my face and I grab hold of her hand, it's the best I can come to a hug right now.

"Shhh, something's going on." Clay says, moving closer to the door with his ear to the metal frame. "They're moving us."

Clay quickly jumps back and the door comes flying open. "Everyone on your fucking feet, we're moving and if you try to fucking slow us down I won't hesitate to put a bullet in each and everyone of your skulls. Move now!" Bull yells at us and pulls out some thick zip ties, the ones cops use when arresting people.

Him and two other men zip tie Clay first then Celine, then Ice and Daria, and lastly me. The second they try to lift me off the floor I throw up a mixture of white foam and blood. I try to drag in a breath, but it feels like an elephant is sitting on my chest.

"I can't. I can't" I fall back down. Daria comes over to me and now I see fear in her eyes.

"We're not leaving here without you. I need you to give me all you got, right fucking now! She orders me and I try to take the strength coming from her, but every movement has me gritting out in pain.

"Move!" Bull screams and I hear a flurry of footfalls outside the door.

We all head up the few stairs leading out of the basement and walk down a steep hill on a trail I can barely see. When we get towards the end of the hill I can see a small dock and a boat house. There's already two airboats waiting there for us.

In the commotion all of the people working with Bull push to get through to one of the boats. In the background I hear the popping sounds of gunfire. Daria's right, it's the boys. The knowledge that we're so close to being saved fills me with a round of adrenaline. We need to do something. I need to do something.

"Ahh!" I collapse in a heap on the rotting wood dock. "Fuck." I groan and roll to my stomach. The girls all stop to help me, probably thinking I'm hurting from my injuries. Clay is the only one standing up.

Bull and most of his men are already on the airboats, the rest are in the boat house.

There are only two guards standing with us. I look up at Clay for a second and pray that he's reading my mind.

When I see him crouch down a little lower I know that he is. I use my leg and kick the one man standing behind us directly in his dick, when he buckles forward Celine clubs him across the face with her tied hands knocking him into the gator infested water.

Clay pushes the other man off the dock in the same fashion and runs to the door of the boat house and holds it closed.

"Get up now! Run. Get them to run now!" He barks at us and I watch as he struggles to keep the door closed.

"No, we can't leave you!" Daria says as we all start backing up.

"If I let this door go, they'll over run us and we won't get away. Go! Now!" He yells at us and just like that we turn and run.

The terrain is so steep that we can't climb back up so we end up having to run along the side. I look back and see Clay finally getting pushed back as a stream of men are coming out after us. He had bought us some time, but if we didn't move fast they'd catch us.

Clay sacrificed himself so we could get away, now we just have to make sure that his sacrifice wasn't in vain.

CHAPTER 19

Pirate

NOAH ENDED UP BACK IN SURGERY, BUT THE information we got from his friend was spot on. We ended up near the old development site and sure enough there are tracks and evidence that people are here. We get through the first row of unfinished houses, but don't see anyone.

It's getting late and the trees have become entwined with some of the building materials making it hard to see if someone is hiding. My eyes focus over the area to the right of me when I see something shine.

"Right." I bark out and everyone swings their guns in that direction.

"What do you see? What is it?" Jameson asks.

Before I have time to say a word a bullet whizzes by my head. "Shit! Danger close!" I call and push Jameson to the ground.

"They're here! Move your ass! We can't let them take the girls anywhere!" Archer orders and while in a crouched position runs in the direction of the person shooting. He gets into the ideal position and stands to take the man out. He's back in motion before the man's body hits the ground.

We run full on sprinting, deeper into the trees waiting to see any signs of someone.

"I hear people! They're down by the marsh area." Bones calls out.

Fuck they're trying to get out on the water. We'd never fucking catch them if they do.

"Get there! Fucking get there!" Archer picks up speed and we all do our best to keep up with him.

I'm still physically fit, but I'm no spring chicken. I fall towards the rear of the group as we push through slippery terrain …

"Mason!" I hear Yang's name sound from the side of us. We're going the wrong way.

"Shit hold! Hold on!" I call out.

"Hold!" Gator calls up to the head of the pack. Archer turns out of breath to me.

"What the fuck are we stopping for?" Jameson thunders.

"Call out!" I command and instantly I hear Isley calling for Mason.

"Ice! Oh fuck, I'm coming!" He takes off in that direction with the rest of us following behind him and almost literally stumbling onto a scene I don't think any of us were prepared for. My heart breaks through the ice that had surrounded it in the past days. I see her. I can see Delia with my own eyes.

I see her and she's hurt.

The women are clawing their way one by one up the side of the hill with a group of Bull's men running trying to catch them.

"Cover them!" Archer commands, and we all open up on the encroaching enemy.

As they back up, we reach down and pull the women up. They cry and hug on us.

"Daria, Come now!" Archer orders her.

"No." She calls back up, then she catches my eyes, "She's not going to make it that way. I'm not leaving her Luke. Find another way!" She says again and holds onto Delia who has barely moved since we got here.

I watch in the distance as two airboats take off and Corrine cries out. "Oh no, Clay!"

"Where is he?" Shyne asks.

Celine is the one to answer, "He was holding them back. He held the door shut so we could get away. They overran him and I didn't see him after that."

I want to be sad about Clay, that my brother is missing, but right now all I can think about is getting to Delia. "Archer, I'm going down." I yell out and go to the edge of the small cliff, there are a few small ledges that I could get down. I jump down and finally when I touch the ground I race with everything I can to her side. She's barely breathing and I can see she is truly fighting for her life.

"Jimmy?" She whimpers.

"Oh sweet girl. I'm so fucking sorry. I'm here. Just stay with me okay. Stay with me here." I coo as Daria is pulled up the side of the cliff by Archer and Lex.

"We're coming brother! We're coming." Lex calls out.

"Hurry up!" I scream at them. She's fading away right in my arms. "Come on baby, please, please, just a little while longer." I push the hair out of her face and her eyes open slightly.

"I have a question." She slurs out.

"What, anything?" I reply, moving closer to her. I don't care what she asks me as long as she keeps talking to me.

She drags in a painful breath and blood gurgles in her mouth. She grips me hard until she can get a breath again. "Will you … marry me?"

Shock and happiness courses through me, "What? Girl, why you taking my job?" I smile at her.

When she gasps again and a tear falls from her eyes, I cradle her closer to me, "Yes, of course I'll marry you. I love you so fucking much. I love you."

She smiles for a second, but her eyes close and a mask of pain takes over. The guys all run over to help me get her up, but I know there is a strong possibility that she won't even make it to the hospital. I'd just got her back and the world is trying to take her away once again.

"Pirate, we have to move. Now!" Bones is screaming in my face, but I don't even remember when he got down here.

"Shyne, you and Lex go down to the pier and see if you find any sign of Clay. Anything." They nod and take off in that direction while the rest of the club huddles around my ol' lady.

I watch as they pick her up, all together and find a safe way to get her over the side of the cliff. The trek back to the trucks is nerve wracking and every step of the way I find myself looking at Delia's chest to make sure she's still breathing.

The girls pile in and we take off leaving Jameson, Celine, and Gator behind to wait on Shyne and Lex.

The minute we get on the main road to the hospital a video comes through to Archer's phone.

Daria is the one to pick it up. When she opens the message she sees a video and immediately starts bawling.

"What! What is it?" Archer says his eyes jerking from the road to her face.

"He's gone, Clay's dead." She turns the phone around, Bull had sent us another video message. In the video we see Clay's body in the shallow water, his kutte clearly visible as the alligators chomp on his body ripping him to pieces.

"Ah fuck." I turn my eyes away. I can't watch that. Clay gave his life for our women, I don't want the last memory I have of him to be the gators going after him. We may have gotten our women, but we'd lost a brother.

CHAPTER 20

Pirate

3 WEEKS LATER

"I SWEAR to God if you try to carry me out of this car I'm never going to talk to you again."

I smile and look at Delia in the rearview mirror. She's pissed, because I'd carried her from the hospital to the car.

I'd carry her for the rest of my life if it means that I'm never going to lose her again. She made it through two surgeries and one hell of an infection to be coming home with me today. My woman is a fighter through and through. I wouldn't have her any other way.

"I guess we're just going to be grunting at each other for a while." I say and she stomps her feet in the well of the truck.

"I hate you!" She growls out.

"Nah, I don't actually believe you." I shrug and pull the truck into one of our spots. I get out of the car and walk over to her side, but she clings to the body of the truck when I open her door.

"Please, Jimmy. Let me be strong on my own. I can do this." She looks up at me and I nod.

"If you wobble once, you're off your feet and in the bed." I wag my finger at her.

She scoffs and gives me a stinky look, "Who the hell died and made you my ruler?"

I watch her cross her arms over her chest and squint at me. I know where this is going and the doctor had already told me that we need to take it easy until her body heals up. I don't think Lia knows the meaning of soft sex.

"Sweet girl, you going to be good for me?" I move closer to talk softly and slowly in her ear. She gasps and grabs hold of my shirt. When I move back to look into those beautiful blue eyes they are full of desire.

"What do I get if I am?" She asks.

"You'll see, I promise it involves you coming several times on my tongue. If you can handle it."

"Fuck, yes!" She hops out of the truck and we walk slowly into the clubhouse.

The minute we do I'm swarmed by all the women pushing me out of the way to get to Delia and make sure she's okay. I don't know how she could ever think she isn't part of this family. We may have broken up, but now it's like she never left.

"Look at you walking and shit." Noah walks up to the small crowd and pulls her into a hug. "We both can't be in the hospital at the same time. There was no one to get my chai lattes." He sighs dramatically and she pulls back to look at him.

"What is this?" She points up to his face that is now covered with a beard, of course its trimmed perfectly. He puts sheen in it and doesn't let anyone touch it like its a fucking baby.

"Oh my bad boy look? After your friends put me back in the hospital I thought I'd let it grow out a bit. Now I'm pretty and fucking rugged, time for me to go knock someone up. It's just the normal progression of these things. I saw a meme on Facebook about it and everything."

Delia laughs and pushes him away. "I'm sorry to inform you Noah, but I think you're going to be getting chai lattes all by yourself from now on. I'm moving out." She tells him and I pull her back against me.

"You're moving out. Does that mean you're coming home now? Are you coming back home to me?"

"Yeah, time for me to be with my family. Besides if we're going to plan that big old wedding I figure we might as well be living in the same place to do it.

She's back.

I can't stop myself from smiling as I bend down and kiss her hard on the mouth. I never want to be away from this woman again. I grab and pick her up while she peppers my face with kisses as I bring her to my … I mean our room.

I can't believe I got a second chance, but now that I have it I'm going to make damn sure that I don't fuck it up.

TWO HOURS after we got home Delia is already sound asleep, safe in bed. I come back down just to be with my family. In the past days shits been hard with the burying of Clay and the women being fearful that someone is going to come for them, all of us have been just trying to get back to normal.

We finally accepted the fact that René is here and he's here to stay. Jameson and Lex are fearful for Celine, but we know that all of us are going to pull together and make sure all of our family stays safe.

I walk over to the bar and Shyne is there handing out drinks, "I get home and everything goes to shit." He jokes.

"It was on the way there way before you came back, but at least you were with us when we needed you." I tell him as I open the beer he's just passed to me.

"Of course, riding nomad with Wire was great and I'll always appreciate him for taking me in and helping to find Tink, but here is home. They're going to have to pry the WOD New Orleans patch out of my dead hands to get me to leave." He tilts his head and clinks his beer with mine before he drinks it. After a second he gestures with his chin over my shoulder.

I turn around to see Noah walking over to me. The cocky smile he usually wears is not on his face any longer. Something's off.

"What's up? You okay?"

"Yeah, It's just I …" He stops talking and just looks down at his feet. I've never known this man to be at a loss for words.

"What?"

"Look, I don't ask for things and I know my personality is a lot. Most people can't fucking deal with me or don't want to, but I feel like maybe you don't hate me as much as most. I rode along with you seeing what this club's about—"

"Stop!" I cut him off and walk away.

I knock on the door to Archer's room. He and Daria have been locked up together the majority of the time since coming home. Any time he's out for more than an hour he's on a mission to get back in that room to her.

He opens the door and I tell him my suggestion quickly. He nods his head and walks out. Archer walks into the middle of the floor on his way to church.

"Noah." He barks out.

I turn to the bar to look for him, but he's not there any longer when I scan the room again I see that he's made his way to the door.

"I think this party is over for me." He answers.

"I don't think so, get your ass over here." Archer looks around to the members that are awake, "Boys, we got business. Time for church."

"Oh shit, new prospect! Fucking finally!" Lex calls out. Gator and Yang come up behind Noah and push him towards the back room where we make all our decisions.

"What the hell is this? I'm not sure if it's orgy time for all of you guys, but I need to be on top. I've got a doctor's note and everything." Noah says, a sly smirk on his face.

Jameson slaps him in the back of his head, and Lex does the same. "Shut up!" The both of them say.

Archer bangs a gavel on the table to call order to the meeting.

Noah opens his mouth like he's going to talk, but I put my hand up to stop him. I just shake my head and put my hands on his back pulling his shoulders so he has to stand up straight. Once church is in session it's not time for jokes.

He takes my hint and gets serious.

"This month has been fucking hard and we can never replace a member like Clay. But we have someone here who has more than shown that he belongs with us, at least in my opinion." Archer says. "I'm proposing to the club that we bring Noah on as a prospect. Let me hear a y—"

"Yeah!" Everyone shouts and claps Noah on the back.

"Shut the hell up! We didn't even ask him yet!" Archer reprimands us. "So what do you say Joker, are you our brother?"

"Joker?" He asks, his eyes getting wide, "Hell yeah!" He says and we laugh at him.

I pull him into a bro hug and let him go for the rest of the guys to congratulate him. If there is anyone who deserves a family it's him. I know he'd give his life for one of us and we'd do the same for him.

I only hope that we can protect him better than we protected Clay.

EPILOGUE
CLAY

Clay

"Fuck! Get the fuck away from me!" I yell out as I sit in the corner of a small room, three chained up dogs bark and snap at me. The chains are long enough that if I move even an inch they'll clamp down on me.

The women got away, I hope they did at least. Bull's men had pulled me in the boat house before I could make sure.

The door opens and the dogs are pulled out of the room.

René walks in and pulls a chair to sit in front of me. "You know I'm not an unreasonable man. I only ask to be given what I'm due. Your club took everything from me, but I'm resilient. I'm going to keep getting back up until my time on this earth is done. Taking the women would have been the end of it. I was getting tired of Archer and the rest of that misfit crew, but you had to go and set them free. Now I don't have my payment. As the sole representative of your club, I hold you responsible."

"I don't give a fuck what you do to me. I promise you they'll come for me. So either you kill me or you get killed, those are your only options." I spit out the words, trying to sound tougher than I am.

"They'll come for you? Oh poor Clay, don't you know. They think you're dead. Archer and the rest of them already held a funeral for you. No one is coming and I don't plan on killing you for a long time. In fact I think I'll set up a five year repayment plan for you. We're going to have a lengthy relationship. I figure I'll start with giving you a little taste of what you guys did to me." He gets up from the chair and pushes it back, "Bull bring it in."

"What the fuck! Get away from me." Bull and three other men come in with a large wood board. They cuff me down, place the board on my legs from the thighs down and slowly one by one stack rocks and small boulders on the board.

"Ahh! No, shit! Stop! Please oh fuck!" I scream and try to move, but the weight is becoming too extreme and I watch in agony as after almost half an hour of them stacking weight on my legs my femur breaks and the head of the bone pushes up into my pelvic area.

"Fuck! Stop! What do you want!" I cry out hard with pain flooding through my body.

"I want nothing. I'll take your pain just on principle, they should have played by the rules." René walks to the door before he turns to one of the men, "Guppie, make sure he doesn't die. If he does revive him. I'll be keeping him for a while." He walks out as the men continue to stack more rocks on and I feel my other leg start to crack under the steady pressure.

The pain pushes my mind into a strange place of numbness and peace. I want to tell myself that I only need to deal with this for a little while. Except if what he said is true and they really think I'm already dead then I'm going to be here for the rest of my life. In agony and alone at the whims of a fucking mad man.

MORE FROM RAE B. LAKE

Wings of Diablo MC

Wire

Archer

Clean

Cherry

Prez

Ryder

Ink

Roth

Mack

Storm

Dillon

Pope

Treble

Wings Of Diablo MC - New Orleans

Jameson

Yang

Bones

Pirate

Shyne

Spawns of Chaos MC

Shepard

Tex

Maino

Nitro

Juric Crime Family

Sven's Mark

Josip's Secret

Kaja's Bet

Luka's Captive

Eve's Fury MC

Becoming Vexx

Free

Riot

Duchess

Sugar

Dark Duet

His Darkest Needs

Her Darkest Gift

Boys of Djinn MC
Wyatt
Cody
Spark

Jagged Peaks
Secret Capture
Buried Memories

The Shop Series Books
His Georgia Peach
To Protect and Serve Donut Holes
On The Edge of Ecstasy
His Peach Sparkle

Royal Bastards MC
Death & Paradise
Chaos & Paradise

Standalones
Drunk Love
Saving Valentine

FOLLOW RAE EVERYWHERE!

FACEBOOK
READER GROUP
TWITTER
INSTAGRAM
GOODREADS
AMAZON
WEBSITE
BOOKBUB
NEWSLETTER
TIKTOK

RAE'S ON KINDLE VELLA

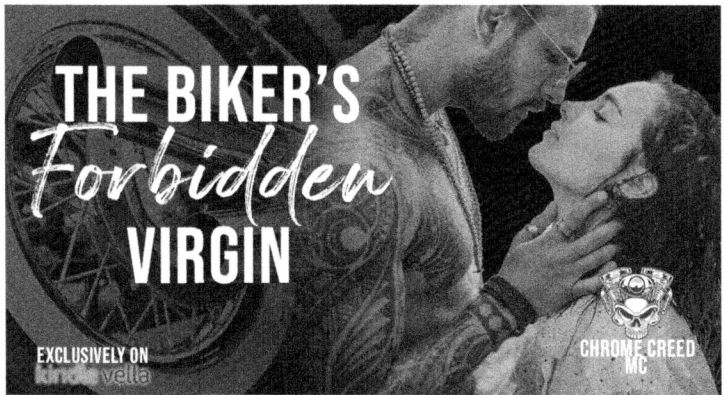

I'm the President of the Chrome Creed MC. A position that comes with privileges. I've never been an easy man, nothing about me soft or slow. I take what I want, hard and fast, until I'm through. Holding back is not something I do until I set my eyes on Nisa. She's young, pure, and not meant for a man like me. Something about her calls to the beast inside me, pushing me past the point of control. I warned her, but she didn't listen. She's completely off-limits. Forbidden. Now she's all mine.

Read it here!

NEXT UP FOR THE WINGS OF DIABLO - NEW ORLEANS CHAPTER

LET'S WELCOME RILEY RAE!

I'd like all of you to get to know one of my alter egos. She's going to be putting out some laugh out loud, alpha hole, bossy, grump romance this new year and she thinks you're just going to love it!

Make sure you follow my Facebook page for updates!

Printed in Great Britain
by Amazon

25893297R00128